UNWILLING VOW

WILLOW FOX

1

OLIVIA

Once you hit rock bottom, nothing matters. Nowhere else to go but up is a lie.

You can always fall harder, faster, farther, straight to Hell.

"Tell me why you're doing this?"

His question catches me off guard. It shouldn't, but I don't have an answer that he'll want to hear. The truth isn't pretty. It's rough and torn around the edges, much like I am.

Broken.

Worn.

Abandoned.

"I need the money," I say.

He'll probably cross me off his little list.

He scribbles something down on his notepad that is situated across his lap. One leg is folded across the other.

He's laid back, comfortable. Hell, the man could be a model.

I'm trying not to bring up my lunch.

His eyes narrow. There's some thought fleeting through his head. I have no idea what it is and whether it involves this interview or he's wondering what he should order for his next meal.

Jace Barone.

Billionaire. Owner and director of Barone Industries.

He owns a bunch of subsidiary companies, but Barone Industries is known for its massive reach into technology for medical, professional, scientific, and innovative purposes. At least that's what I read in the brochure on my way up to his office.

His smile is tight-lipped. He's barely looked at my resume, unimpressed.

"You have children at home?"

Excuse me? What kind of question is that for a job interview?

I purse my lips together. It's none of his business. "No."

"But you've done this before?" Jace asks.

He closes his leather binder containing his notepad and fiddles with his pen, tapping it against the black leather grain. "Usually, the interviewee explains why they should be chosen, what they have to offer, aside from looks."

How dare he!

I want to wipe the smug look right off his face.

"Listen, I'm sorry. It was a mistake coming here," I say and stand. It wasn't entirely my choice, but I'm here, and I need a job, but I can't be an assistant to an asshole billionaire. I have no experience, and he's highly unprofessional. Shockingly, he hasn't been sued.

His interview skills are significantly lacking and make me more than slightly uncomfortable.

"Sit back down," Jace growls at me.

I slump back into the chair. I can't imagine he's going to hire me.

Is this to torture me? There's desperate, and then there's pathetic.

I'm feeling like the latter.

He places his leather folder on the desk in front of him and clasps his hands together. "I apologize if I'm a bit on edge. My personal life has been an uphill battle these past few weeks," Jace says.

I force a smile. "It's fine."

"It's not, but I appreciate your consideration," he says. "Now, I want to know why you'd like to carry my child."

The color disappears from my face. The room spins, and the next thing I know, all I see is darkness.

2

JACE

Did she seriously just faint during the surrogacy interview?

Interviewing at my office was a bad idea. I can't believe Matteo, my second in command, this was his idea.

I should fire his ass.

One second, I'm talking, and she doesn't appear to be paying attention to me. The faraway distant look made my stomach knot.

I've seen that look before.

My younger sister faints a lot. Unlike most people, I've learned to see the signs.

I leap out of my chair and catch Olivia on her way down to the ground before she can hit her head.

She blinks several times, staring up at me.

With her lying on the ground, I pull out my phone to call 9-1-1.

"That's embarrassing," she mutters under her breath. Olivia tries to pull away from me to stand.

"Just sit tight," I say. "I'm calling an ambulance. You just passed out."

"I'm fine," she says as she sits up. "Please don't call an ambulance."

It's hard not to worry, and I can't afford to get sued. I don't let her stand.

"Just stay there," I insist. I crouch down to her level, keeping a close eye on her. The color is slowly coming back to her cheeks. I grab a bottle of water off my desk. It's still sealed from this morning. I haven't opened it for myself yet.

I twist the top off and hand it to her. "Drink," I command. She needs to stay hydrated.

Her hands tremble as she brings the bottle to her lips.

"Do you pass out a lot?" I'm trying to make small talk. There's no way she can be the surrogate for my child if she has health issues that lead her to pass out randomly in strange places.

She shakes her head and winces. "No, I didn't eat breakfast."

I glance at the clock on the wall. It's nearly four in the afternoon. "What about lunch?"

She smiles, tight-lipped. "Skipped it."

Why the hell hasn't she eaten anything all day? "I think we've discovered the culprit," I say.

How can she skip two meals? Is she worried about her weight? I try not to glance her over, but she's got luscious curves. She doesn't look like she's starving herself, but what do I know? I've barely spent twenty minutes with this woman.

I reach for my phone, and she places a hand on my wrist. "Please, I can't afford the medical bills."

There's desperation behind her tone. "Let me message one of my employees to get you something to eat," I say. "It's on me. Okay?"

She reluctantly nods.

Good, I'm glad I don't have to argue with her and convince her to sit tight while I have to force a meal down her throat. That would be far less comfortable.

I cancel the original call and text Matteo.

Grab me some orange juice and a sandwich. The 3:30 just fainted in my office.

Matteo is typing back. Three dots flash on the screen before my stomach flops.

Your 3:30 surrogacy appointment was canceled a few hours ago.

Then who the hell is the girl in my office?

3

YESTERDAY MORNING

OLIVIA

There's a sharp knock on my car window, startling me from slumber.

I slept in my vehicle, in the Walmart parking lot.

It's morning and sunny out. It takes a few moments for my vision to adjust to the brightness.

Shit, it's the mafia.

Luka Caruso, he's don for the Caruso family. The big boss. Why the hell doesn't one of his guys harass me instead?

Luka likes to make it known that he's in charge of this city.

My husband, John, did business with the Carusos. Lucky me, John is dead, but he never paid his debt, and it's been handed down to me.

Even in death, my husband screwed me over. He was a shitty husband, but he didn't deserve to die. Late at night, sometimes I wonder if Luka Caruso is to blame for John's death.

I roll down my window. It's not like I have a choice in the matter. Even if I run, Luka will find me.

My mouth is dry and I worry what he might do to me. Will he cut off my fingers? Set my car ablaze?

"I don't have it. As soon as I get a job, I'll pay you back," I say, desperate.

Can't he tell that I'm living in my car? It's not like I'm driving a new sports car and sleeping in a mansion.

He pulls out a business card. "You have an interview tomorrow. If he asks, tell him that your friend Avery Seymore sent you."

"You know Avery?" I ask. My stomach tenses. Is she in their debt, too? I haven't seen her since the funeral, Austin's.

He doesn't answer my question.

Why would I expect him to tell me anything? I'm lucky he hasn't put a bullet in my head yet. He will if I don't pay him back for my late husband's debts.

How much of the city does the Caruso family own?

I should run. Leave town. Get out while I still can, while I'm alive. These men don't play games. They murder innocent people.

I glance at the business card for Barone Industries. Everyone has heard of the company. They're one of the top five organizations in the world.

"What kind of job is it?" I have a resume, but it's not like I have a ton of work experience.

"Does it matter? You owe the Carusos, and we've come to collect. Convince Jace Barone to hire you, and we'll let you live."

"The billionaire?" I squeak. It's no secret he's one of the world's richest men. How am I going to convince him to hire me?

What can I offer him that no other candidate can?

4

OLIVIA

There's a shift in Jace Barone's demeanor. His eyes flicker as he reads the text message on his screen.

"It's really no bother. I can go," I say. I probably shouldn't have admitted that I hadn't eaten anything all day. It's not that I didn't have time or didn't want to eat.

I didn't have the money.

My wallet is empty. And I've been living out of my car for the past two weeks since I've been evicted. Not that he needs to know that. I'm not here for a handout.

I'm here for a job and to fix an already bad situation, not make it worse.

I press my hands flat on the floor and intend on standing.

"Sit back down," he commands.

"So, I guess the job is out of the question?" I laugh nervously and roll my lips together.

He runs a hand through his thick, dark hair. His dark green eyes bore into mine. I hate to admit it, but he's devilishly handsome. Much hotter than my last fling, which put a baby into me. He left the minute I got pregnant and then came running back to marry me once the kid was born and he lost his job.

Talk about real love.

It sucks.

"Job," he says and stares at me. His eyes tighten, and there's that strange flicker again. His dark green irises have speckles of amber and gold mixed in. It's hypnotizing his gaze. "What job do you think you're here for again?" he asks.

"Now, who hit their head?" I ask.

Is he testing me and making sure that I'm coherent after the fainting spell?

"An assistant position with your organization, Barone Industries," I say. "My friend, Avery Seymore, told me about the opening." I recant exactly what Don Caruso told me to say.

Jace can't know that I'm consorting with the mafia.

No one can know the truth.

"Assistant," he mulls over the words and strokes his jaw. "I do need an assistant, but I wasn't aware we were hiring anyone from the outside." He shakes his head. "I don't know an Avery, and I have to apologize for what probably felt like an interrogation earlier."

"A quite inappropriate one, I might add," I say.

Does he realize the type of questions that he asked could get him in hot water? Anyone else and they'd have been fired over his questions.

There's a firm knock at the door.

"Come in," Jace says.

Another striking gentleman in a business suit, perhaps a few years younger than Jace but not by much, brings in a wrapped deli sandwich, bottle of orange juice, and a bag of potato chips. It looks like he stopped in the cafeteria and grabbed a pre-made sandwich.

It looks delicious.

My mouth waters at the sight of it.

Maybe I can take the sandwich and scram. I don't want to be under his scrutiny or answer any more of his inappropriate and awkward questions.

"How about you have a seat at my desk?" Jace asks.

The gentleman bringing in the food gives Jace a peculiar look. He looks older than I'd expect from an assistant. Maybe that's why they're hiring for the position?

"That isn't necessary," I say. I want to leave as quickly as I can, but I get the feeling he's not going to let me leave until he says I can go.

"I wasn't asking," Jace says.

He helps me to my feet, one arm around my waist, the other on my arm as he practically lifts me.

I feel lightheaded, not that I admit it to him. The last time I had bouts of dizziness was after the funeral.

Jace keeps his hold on me, probably making sure I don't fall. I'd be a huge liability if I got hurt, and while he's a billionaire, I'm sure he doesn't want to have to pay me to go away and never speak about it.

He doesn't stay a billionaire by throwing his money around.

Jace escorts me to his enormous leather chair and makes me sit at his desk.

The material is soft and cool. It's far more comfortable than I could have imagined. The chair probably costs more than the current value of my car parked outside.

Once he's confident that I'm not going to fall, he glides the chair closer to the desk and swipes at the papers, putting anything confidential into his desk drawer, locking it after he's done.

The key, on his keyring, slides back into his pocket.

The other gentleman places the food on Jace's desk.

It's a bit of overkill, but I reach for the orange juice first. My hands shake, and I fumble with the lid.

Jace takes the bottle from me, opens it, and hands it back.

I smile sheepishly. "Thanks."

"Boss," the other gentleman says and nods toward the door.

"I have some things to deal with. Can you sit here, eat your lunch, and not get into trouble?" Jace asks.

I feel like he's talking to me as if I were a young child. He is putting himself out for me, though, so I nod and take a sip of my orange juice. I don't want to overstay my welcome. I want to leave, but he's probably right. If I pass out in the elevator, who is going to help me down to the car?

And I can't afford an ambulance ride, let alone a massive bill from the hospital, which is what I would get without insurance.

Jace retreats from the office, closing the door.

He's standing on the opposite side. I have no clue what he's saying, but he's quite animated with his colleague.

Jace looks pissed.

Is it because of me?

Is he upset that the gentleman took a few minutes to grab me something to eat? I don't want to be an imposition.

I unwrap the sandwich. While I want to savor every bite, I can't. I'm starving.

A turkey sandwich never tasted so delicious in my life. I don't care that the bread is cold, slightly stale, and dry.

I gulp the orange juice between bites. The taste is rich and thick. Sweet like molasses. Best of all, there isn't any pulp. However, I wouldn't be particularly picky.

Already, my head feels attached again, and the dizziness vanishes with each passing minute as I devour my free meal.

As soon as I finish my lunch, I'll head out. Hopefully, he won't be by the door, and I can sneak out, never to see him again.

5

JACE

"Who's the girl?" Matteo asks.

I'm standing across from him just outside my office. I can see Olivia through the open blinds. The blinds were added at my insistence, to give a modicum of privacy, but now I realize there's hardly any privacy at all.

"Olivia Summers. She thought she was interviewing for an assistant position," I say and rake my fingers through my hair.

How the hell did this get screwed up?

Matteo's cheeks burn. "I fucked up, boss. I should have told you directly that your interview was canceled."

"Who the hell sent Ms. Summers upstairs to my office?" I'm about ready to have their head.

"I'll find out for you, sir," Matteo says.

I exhale a heavy puff of air, staring at the girl seated at my desk.

No one ever sits in Don Barone's chair.

Ever.

But the longer I stare at her through the blinds, the more I realize I want her.

Not for an assistant. And certainly not intimately.

Don't get me wrong, she's hot, with a rocking, curvy body, but I don't mix business with pleasure. The last thing I need is some girl learning my deep, dark secrets.

They're secrets for a reason.

I hardly ever date as it is. There are too many women out there looking to chase after my money. It's easier to play the field.

Safer.

Cheaper.

I don't need a girlfriend hanging on my arm at functions. I'm the boss of Barone Industries. Who the hell do I have to impress? No one.

"I want her," I say, staring at her through the window.

"Excuse me?" Matteo says and clears his throat. He's expecting me to say something else and pretends he didn't hear what I said.

No, he heard me correctly.

"I want her as my surrogate."

"Sir, you can't just go in there and—"

"The hell I can't. I'm Jace Barone." I do whatever the hell I damn well please. It helps that I have more money than I need, and I get the feeling the little tiger in there is desperate for a job.

Except it's not the job she came in here hoping to get hired for.

"Think about what you're suggesting, sir," Matteo says.

He's always levelheaded. Calm.

I'm impulsive.

He's the yin to my yang. It's what makes him a great second.

But I'm the boss, not Matteo. Which means even my worst ideas I can see through. No one can fire me. Sure, I have a board of directors whom I have to deal with, but I'm not suggesting that this little tiger come and work for me professionally.

Though it's not the worst idea.

Sleeping with her, burying my cock inside her tightness, is the absolute worst idea.

And fuck it if I can't keep a clear head.

Most women chase me. The fact that she seems immune to who I am, it's sexy as hell.

Hell, she's sexy. Just the way she carries herself and isn't afraid to speak freely. That's hot as sin.

I return my attention to Matteo. He can object all he wants. I always get my way.

"I have contract lawyers who can ensure everything will go smoothly."

"Even so, to even make such a suggestion could be grounds for a lawsuit. The woman came into your office for an assistant position and then you suggested she become a surrogate. We've been using an agency. Don't you think it's best if we continue to do things as we have been?"

He can tell the agency to go fuck themselves. No one notified me that the surrogate had canceled our appointment. They should have reached out to me directly, not my second, Matteo. It was probably an oversight, but one that is a problem.

"I think I should ask her before dismissing the idea entirely," I say, staring at Matteo.

I fail to hear the office door open.

Olivia steps out, her pale blue eyes wide and bright. She tucks a strand of her strawberry blonde hair behind her ear. She's beautiful.

Stunning.

I can imagine the perfect mix of our children. While I hope it's a boy to carry on my legacy, I'd even be happy with a little girl who would resemble her.

She's what I've been looking for.

While unconventional at best, I'll give her a choice.

The decision is entirely up to her.

But I always get what I want.

"Thank you for lunch. I should head out," Olivia says, glancing between me and Matteo. Her shoulders are slumped. She's trying to be invisible, but that's not possible.

I could never forget a woman like her, and we've just met.

"Before you leave," I say and rest my hand on her arm. I guide her back into my office and shut the door before Matteo can interrupt.

I'm sure he's biting his tongue, wanting to scream how bad an idea this is. I'm no idiot. I never thought it was ideal, but sometimes things happen. Opportunities fall at your feet on your doorstep, and you have to take them.

I'm giving her that opportunity.

The chance of a lifetime.

"I don't want to take up any more of your time. I'm sure you're busy, and you've already been too kind," Olivia says. She's fumbling with her words.

There's a nervousness to her exterior, which is sweet, endearing. In another life, we might have had a chance.

But I'm not that man, the sweet, wholesome husband.

I can't be that man.

I'll never be him. I've accepted my role, my fate. I've spent my life focusing on my organization, both Barone Industries and the family, the men I support.

There's no room for a wife or queen on the throne.

"I have an offer that I'd like to make you," I say and clear my throat.

Olivia's eyes widen. They're the brightest blue that I've ever seen. They sparkle from the reflection of the floor-to-ceiling windows overlooking the Pacific Ocean. It's sunny outside. Blindingly so today.

"You're offering me the assistant job?" she asks.

"No," I say. I keep my voice calm and collected. I don't want to lead her on in any way. "Have a seat." I gesture to the chair that she was in earlier for the interview.

I perch myself at the edge of my desk while she sits. This way, I'm close enough if she has another fainting spell that I ensure I'll catch her.

"Do you faint very often?" I ask.

Her brow furrows. "No, this is the first time that I've ever passed out," Olivia says. "I'm sorry. What does this have to do with the offer that you're making?"

It's no wonder she's confused. I haven't spelled things out for her. "I am looking to hire a surrogate," I say.

"Let me guess. You aren't hiring an assistant?" Olivia asks, disappointment all over her face.

"Not at this time," I say. I clasp my hands together in front of me. "I am searching for a woman who would be willing to carry my child. Have you had kids before?"

"You're asking me to be the surrogate?" Olivia coughs, and I reach for the bottle of water from earlier, offering it to her. "I'm sorry. I'm just a little flustered. I didn't expect that type of offer."

"I'd be willing to pay the surrogate fifty thousand dollars per month, along with a healthy stipend for maternity clothes and any other necessities. Medical care would be paid and provided for by my physician of choice. I want the best for my child."

She pulls her bottom lip between her teeth.

I've made her uncomfortable. I should have seen that coming. I'm not an idiot, but asking her was downright stupid.

"Have you had children before?" I ask.

It's a requirement with the surrogate agency for a woman to have had at least one healthy, full-term pregnancy and delivery.

"Yes, a son," she whispers. "He's, uh, with his father."

I glance at her hand. "You're divorced?" I don't see a ring on her finger.

Her eyes tighten, but she doesn't answer.

It's unusual for a father to have full custody.

Could she not afford a good lawyer? I want to help her.

Matteo would scream at me to back off and leave well enough alone. But I can't do that. I don't want to do that.

"How about I let you think it over," I say. I retrieve a business card from my wallet and flip it over, scribbling my cell phone number on the back.

I hand her the card, and she exhales a shaky breath.

"Let me know what you decide."

Wordlessly, she takes the card from me.

I escort her out of my office and to the elevator, ensuring she finds her way downstairs. I press the down button, and she stands there, staring at the card.

The elevator dings, and she steps inside.

"Just think about it."

6

OLIVIA

I must be crazy for considering his request.

He wants me to be a surrogate for his child.

That's insane.

I should have told him no. Flat out refused on the spot. I'm not a baby-making factory for some billionaire who wants a kid.

But the pay is more than I could earn in a year and that's for just one month. Nine months pregnant is a lot of money for a temporary gig. Maybe if I start thinking about it as a temporary job, it'll be easier to unravel in my head.

The minute I step outside the building, I dig out my cell phone and dial Harper.

I haven't spoken with her in a few weeks. We used to be best friends as kids. She moved to Breckenridge to be with the hot bodyguard she met while filming a feature film. They settled down and started a family.

I've neglected to keep in touch with her. Plus, she's been busy with her famous Hollywood lifestyle. But we always call on each other's birthdays and Christmas.

If she knew the trouble I was in with the mafia and living out of my car, she'd fly into Los Angeles and save my ass.

But I don't need saving, and I'm not looking for a handout.

Jace Barone didn't say that I had to keep his offer a secret. I mean, even if he did, someone would inevitably find out that he has a kid.

It will be front-page news.

He's always on the news, constantly being bombarded by the media.

My stomach somersaults.

Is that what I have to look forward to if I say yes? Jace is famous, and the spotlight seems to follow him around. Both good and bad.

I ring Harper, but she doesn't answer. I leave her a brief message, demanding that she call me back ASAP. I don't indicate why. It's not like I think the phones are tapped, but how would I tell her that one of the world's richest men asked me to carry his child as a surrogate? That's a mouthful and likely to give her a heart attack.

Walking toward my car, I flip over the business card, staring at his name in gold letters glittering under the afternoon sun.

"You really want me to have your kid?" I mutter to myself.

Am I crazy for thinking that I might go through with it?

There's a lot of money involved, and I've been living in my car. I'd be crazy to say no. Of course, it's even more insane for me to agree.

I unlock my car and sit in the front seat. I turn the business card over and dial his number. I haven't even been gone ten minutes, but I can't take the chance he'll change his mind.

I need the money, and this is the best opportunity for a fresh start. After I'm done, I can take the cash and leave this city behind. Then, I'll drive to Breckenridge and see my old high school friend. We were practically inseparable. Houses have to be cheaper in the middle of nowhere, Montana.

Life must be simpler, too.

It'll be perfect.

I dial his phone number and expect it to go to voice mail. He's the CEO of a billionaire dollar enterprise. I doubt he has time to take my call.

He answers on the first ring. "This is Jace."

I can't lose my nerve. I'm ready to hang up. My stomach sinks and my heart leaps out of my chest. I might vomit.

"Hello?" he says, met with my silence.

It takes every ounce of strength to muster up the courage to speak. "I'll do it," I whisper.

"Olivia?"

Of course, he doesn't recognize my number or my voice, either. "Yes, it's Olivia Summers. I'll do it," I say.

I swear there's a smile on his face. Maybe I just imagine it.

"Good. I'll need you to come by and fill out some paperwork."

"At your office?" I ask, my voice squeaking.

I haven't left yet. I could march back inside and handle all the tedious stuff now. The sooner, the better. I want to put a roof over my head.

"No, my house," he says. "I'll text you the address. How about on Monday afternoon or evening?"

That's four days away.

It feels like a lifetime. I have no money in my wallet, and my gas tank is getting low—four days without a decent meal. I should have saved half of the sandwich he gave me.

"Any chance we can do it sooner?" Maybe I can convince him to give me an advance on my pay. I desperately need the money, and I'm not going to get pregnant overnight. That isn't how this works.

"Is Monday not good for your schedule? I'll reach out to my attorney and have him finalize the paperwork," Jace says. He's all business. I can't imagine him being a father. He seems too busy with Barone Industries to raise a child, but busy men have kids.

"Maybe we could meet tonight to discuss the specifics. I've never been a surrogate before, and other than the basics of carrying a pregnancy to term, I don't know what you're expecting of me."

"Fair enough. Come by tonight around eight. I'll text you the address. We can go over the particulars along with any questions that you have."

I breathe a sigh of relief. "Great."

Maybe I can sneak some food out of his fridge while I'm over at his house.

7

JACE

"You shouldn't have asked her to be a surrogate," Matteo says. He folds his arms across his chest. "It's a lawsuit waiting to happen."

I shut my office door so that no one else can overhear the conversation between us.

"I'm aware of the risks. But the girl, she's obviously in trouble." Besides, it's his fault this happened. If he hadn't suggested having the agency schedule an appointment at my office, there never would have been a misunderstanding.

I blame Matteo.

"And you think offering her to be a surrogate and throwing thousands of dollars at her is what, the answer to her problems?"

"Money solves a lot of problems," I say. "There are men who would kill me for my position."

Matteo rolls his eyes. "Not because you're the CEO of this place."

I glare at him to watch his tone. Not that there's surveillance or the place is bugged, but you can never be too careful.

I don't only run a corporation; I also run the mafia. I'm the head of the family. My men call me Don Barone.

"Anyway, she called and said yes. I've agreed to meet with her this evening to go over my expectations and make sure that she's onboard one hundred percent before signing the paperwork."

I approach my desk and unlock the drawer, retrieving the manila folder along with the leather binder I had doodled on during her interview.

"You're not the least bit worried that this is a setup?" Matteo asks.

He's always a little on the paranoid side. He's a good man, trustworthy, but his instincts are only on point about half the time. He's like a brother to me, but I don't have any biological brothers.

I only have a sister, who's six years younger. We don't talk. She hates what I do for a living, despises me. I'm not too crazy about her, either.

A frown etches across my face. "A setup. How, exactly? She came in for an assistant position."

"Yes, an assistant position that doesn't exist."

"You didn't bring her in? You're always blabbing on about hiring me an assistant around here. How I need someone to make sure I don't miss a board meeting and can send out and answer emails for me."

"Well, I may have mentioned it to HR, but I'm sure that I explained it would be an internal position. Not someone right off the street," Matteo says.

I flip open the leather binder and glance down at the name I jotted during the interview with Olivia. "Do you know an Avery Seymore?"

"Yes, she works in the accounting department," Matteo says. "She's a level one, been around for maybe three years. Young, bright, a little too enthusiastic, but she's a hard worker."

"Olivia mentioned her name during the interview. She must have told her about the assistant position." I'm still perplexed by how our wires got crossed.

"That is my fault, and I assure you that it won't happen again."

I shut the leather binder. "Good."

———

I pick up dinner on my way home. It's nearly eight, and I don't have time to cook a healthy meal, certainly not before company comes over.

That company is Olivia Summers.

My hands are sweaty, and my stomach is bubbling.

Why am I nervous?

She could turn me down, throw a lawsuit at me, or humiliate me and try to destroy the reputation that I've built.

But that's not what I find unsettling.

It's the five foot five inches of perfection from a woman I've barely spent any time with. She stirs a desire inside me that I can't explain. There's a line I won't be able to cross with her.

Sex is off the table.

The previous surrogates I interviewed, I never would have even considered crossing that line.

But I also decided against each of them. One was married. The second had been a journalist attempting to get a story.

They didn't fit the image ingrained in my mind of what I wanted.

"Do you honestly think a traditional surrogate is a way to go?" Matteo asks. "She could claim a right to the child, and things could get messy. No offense, boss, but you're rich as fuck. Any woman could easily take advantage of your generosity."

Does he think I'm an idiot?

"And why do you think I'm doing this through surrogacy instead of knocking up the next girl I bed? I'm being cautious." I sweep the papers of candidates to the side of my desk.

Matteo stands on the opposite side as I sit behind the desk in my leather chair.

Comfortable.

Although I'm not the least bit relaxed.

I've been stressed thinking about the fact that I have no heir. No child to inherit my name or run the Barone family when I'm gone. While I don't intend that day to be any time soon, I would like to know I have a son who will follow in my footsteps.

"These candidates are garbage," I say, pinning Matteo with my stare. "Anyone can lie on paper."

"Sir—" Matteo says, and I cut him off. I don't want his excuses.

There's only one way for me to feel confident that the surrogate is right.

Half my child's DNA will be coming from the mother. I can't depend on statistics and accomplishments from an egg donor.

I need to see the mother for myself, determine if she's a good fit and if my child could benefit from her genetics.

It's not about hair color or the shade of her eyes. Those things don't matter to me.

There's stubbornness and tenacity that I'm looking for in a woman—a fire and a spark that won't diminish. I need an heir who won't cower toward the enemy.

That type of personality doesn't reveal itself on a piece of paper.

"I want to meet the surrogate, spend time with her, know without a doubt that she is the right person to give me a child."

"Did I mention that I'm against this, boss?"

"Repeatedly."

A dark blue hatchback is parked out front by the street.

I drive past but don't see anyone in the driver's seat. I press the buzzer, open the wrought-iron gates, and pull into the driveway.

I glance in the rearview, ensuring the metal gates are closing before I pull around into the garage and shut the doors.

Stepping out of the car, I grab the takeout food and head inside the house.

The lights flip on automatically.

I disarm the alarm and head to the kitchen to grab dishes, silverware, and something to drink.

It's not quite eight o'clock yet, but it has to be Olivia's car parked out front. I don't recognize the vehicle, and it is old and battered. She could use the money from being a surrogate to get herself a new set of wheels.

Maybe I can sweeten the deal if she's on the fence. Offer to buy her a car.

Would that be crossing the line?

Like I haven't already been inappropriate by suggesting she become a surrogate.

I pinch the bridge of my nose.

Sometimes I speak before I think. It's a bad trait that could destroy me. In my case, it's gotten me most of what I wanted out of life. And the few things it hasn't, well, I have my family to help me with that.

My mafia family.

My biological family is dead to me. Well, my sister, that is, she's all that's left of the Barone's, and she betrayed me.

I leave the bag of food on the table and head outside. Did Olivia take a walk?

After I unlock the gate, I step outside and notice her head pop up from the backseat.

Was she sleeping in her car?

I approach her vehicle as she opens the back door and climbs out. She has quite a bit of clothes in the backseat, a pillow and blanket too.

"Are you living in your car?" I ask.

Her cheeks burn as she glances past me, avoiding eye contact. "No, I was just taking a nap until it was time for our meeting," Olivia says.

"Come on inside," I say and usher her through the open gate and into the house. "I brought dinner home. There's plenty, and I'll make you a plate."

"That isn't necessary," Olivia says.

"Have you eaten dinner already?" I lock up the house, arming the alarm before grabbing a second plate for her.

"Uh, no. Not yet. It's fine. I had a big lunch." Her eyes widen when she realizes what she said. "I mean, the sandwich I had was only a few hours ago."

"You'll eat with me." I pull out the takeout containers, open the plastic lids, and lay them out on the counter. I grab enough spoons, one for each dish, and then make myself a plate.

Olivia stands there, staring at the food.

Is she not going to help herself?

"Here," I hand her the plate that I intended for myself and quickly dish out dinner onto a second plate for myself.

If she's shy, she doesn't need to be.

"Come, sit at the table." I walk her into the dining room, bringing two bottles of water with me.

The thought of alcohol fleets through my mind, but I want her to be sober for our discussion.

"Thank you for dinner," she says as she sits. "You didn't have to do that."

I get the feeling that she wouldn't have eaten if I didn't. "It isn't a problem," I insist. "Tell me, Olivia, what makes you want to be a surrogate?" I need to know that she's not doing this only for the money. That she wants to carry my child. It's no easy feat.

Her gaze is on her meal as she hungrily devours the food on her plate. "I should probably tell you what you want to hear, how I can give you something that you can't do on your own. The joy of bringing a life into this world. How I can gift you something that money can't compare to, but the truth is my reasons are more selfish."

"So, it is about the money."

I need her honesty, and my stare meets hers.

"Yes. No," she says, fumbling with her words.

"Which is it?" I ask, studying her.

I want the truth.

She tucks a strand of hair behind her ear and glances up briefly before taking another bite of dinner, this time working on her vegetables.

The veggies were a bit bland for my taste, overcooked, and not that good.

She's eating them like she doesn't know when she'll get her next meal.

Is she homeless? Or just has a healthy appetite? She only had a sandwich and a bag of chips earlier. Hardly much for an entire day's worth of calories.

Unless is she already pregnant? Because that would be a problem. However, the doctor will give her a thorough exam and physical before starting the procedure.

"I miss my son. Doing this isn't completely selfless. Pregnancy was one of my favorite times with my boy."

"He's with his father."

She mentioned that earlier at the office. I can't imagine what type of man keeps his child from his mother. Olivia doesn't appear to be unstable, except perhaps financially.

Is that why she doesn't have guardianship of her son?

She reaches for her water and takes a sip. I can't tell if she's avoiding my remark or thirsty. It's probably a sensitive subject. It would be for me if someone else had custody of my child, which will never happen.

Another reason not to have a traditional style relationship.

"What do I need to know?" Olivia asks.

I sit across from her, finishing the last of my dinner. "You'll be required to undergo medical testing to ensure that you're not already pregnant and that you're healthy."

"And you'll be paying for that?" Her voice is soft, tentative. She sounds nervous.

Is it because I intimidate her, or she has something to hide?

I take a sip of water and nod. "Yes, all your expenses will be covered. Where are you living?" I ask.

Her eyes widen, and she reaches for her water. "With a friend."

She doesn't meet my stare.

I don't believe her. The pillow and blanket in her car are apparent signs of distress. "I will set you up with an apartment."

"I won't be able to afford—"

I interrupt her before she can finish. "I'm handling the expenses."

"That is quite generous of you, sir."

"Jace," I say. "Call me Jace. You'll stay in the apartment until you're pregnant with my child. At which point, after the first trimester, I will expect you to live here, under my roof. You will, of course, be provided your own bedroom and bathroom."

"You expect me to move in with you?" Her tongue darts out and swipes across her cherry lips. Her cheeks redden as she speaks.

"It is part of the arrangement," I explain. "I assure you that you will have your privacy, but I do want to be part of the experience of having a child."

She straightens her shoulders and exhales a soft breath. The nervousness seems to dispel from her body. "That's not typically how surrogacy works." Her tone is stronger, much bolder.

She's not wrong, but I'm also not the typical guy, either. Does she need a reminder of what I'm offering? Will that entice her into saying yes?

"You're right. However, most surrogates also make twenty-five thousand dollars total. I'm offering double that amount per month."

Did she think there'd be no strings attached to the money and that I'd pay her an exorbitant sum of money just because I'm wealthy?

Olivia sucks in a sharp breath. Her cheeks are as red as her lips, and she looks quite a bit flushed. The room isn't overly warm or uncomfortable. "About the money. Are you expecting anything intimate to happen between us?"

I smile. Maybe the blush is from her question.

Does she want something intimate to happen between us?

I can't deny that she is attractive, but I can refuse to act on those desires.

"No, as I explained, you will have your own bedroom. I just want you and my child under my roof. I want my son to recognize my voice."

"Or daughter," Olivia whispers.

"Yes, or daughter." While I want a boy, I will be content with either. A girl will just mean that I may have to hire a surrogate again.

"I will require you to sign over your parental rights. I have a lawyer drawing up the papers." I can't take the chance that she'll change her mind and decide that she wants custody of the child. "Is there anything else you want out of the arrangement?" I ask.

For a woman who previously lost custody of her child, I would assume that she'd seek legal counsel and ask for my help. I know the best lawyers in Los Angeles.

"You're already being quite generous," she says. "I hate even asking, but is it possible that I could have an advance, at least a partial one? My gas tank in my car is low and—"

I hold up a hand, stopping her from finishing her sentence. "Tonight, you'll stay in the guest bedroom. Tomorrow, I will have you moved into one of the apartments that we own. We will get you a small stipend in advance to cover minor expenses until everything is finalized."

I'm not a monster, but I also won't be taken advantage of, either.

8

OLIVIA

I retire for the night not long after dinner and our discussion about surrogacy.

He shows me to the bathroom, and I'm relieved for a hot shower. I've been using the campground facilities to bathe. It's quite a drive away from the city, which hasn't helped me conserve fuel.

The shower is heavenly. Hot water pours over me. I take longer than I should and eventually wash every bit of grime from my skin. I'm not that dirty physically, but I feel disgusting until it all swirls down the drain.

I climb under the covers. The bed is firm, and the sheets are cool.

There's a silence that fills the room, with no traffic constantly passing by the road.

There are no sounds at all. It's hard to fall asleep at first, in an unfamiliar bedroom, but it's nice to have a bed and not have to sleep in my car.

I was too afraid to ask how much I would owe Jace if I can't conceive. I'm still considerably young, twenty-four, and should be able to have another child.

But what if I can't?

What if I don't get pregnant?

————

I awaken the following day. The house smells of bacon and eggs. Climbing out of bed, I scamper down the stairs to the kitchen.

For a billionaire, his house is relatively normal. It's bigger than my apartment where I used to live, but the place isn't probably more than two thousand square feet. Modest for a man who makes more money in one month than I will in my lifetime.

"Good morning," Jace says, standing in front of the stove. He's in dark blue sweatpants and a white t-shirt.

He looks sexy.

But I can't let my thoughts go there. That's a bad idea. This is strictly business, nothing more, and the chance for a fresh start.

"Morning," I say. "I thought you'd be at work already."

"I'll go in a little later this morning. I want to make sure you get settled into your apartment this morning. Matteo is going to swing by here with the keys to your place."

"Oh, that's nice of him."

I have no idea who Matteo is, but I'm glad I will have a roof over my head.

"Also, my lawyer texted me this morning and can have the papers ready by the end of the business day. If you want to meet tonight, we can go over them together and sign the documents."

"Yeah, sure," I say.

I don't have anywhere else to be. The sooner, the better.

"Do you mind if I grab something to drink?" I ask.

"There's orange juice, milk, and water in the fridge. Coffee is in the carafe."

"Cups for coffee are where?" I ask. I'm unfamiliar with the layout of his kitchen, where he keeps everything stocked.

He strides quickly to the coffee pot and, above it, opens the cabinet, retrieving a mug. "Here." He hurries back to the stove, flipping the bacon.

"Thanks," I say.

I pour a mug of coffee and open the fridge, grabbing a bottle of flavored creamer. My favorite. It's like the man knows the way straight to my heart.

"I do have one concern about the agreement." While I haven't seen it yet, I need to know that I won't be on the line for thousands of dollars, owing him money if I can't conceive.

"Yes?" he asks, glancing at me.

He's waiting for me to elaborate.

I'm going to be sick. Bile rises to my throat.

I swallow back my nerves and sip the scorching hot liquid. The bitterness is a welcome treat. "If I can't conceive, will I owe you for the apartment, medical expenses, all that you're doing for me?"

I can't look at him.

I stare into my mug, my eyes down toward the floor, embarrassed that I can't afford to take care of myself.

Jace sighs and puts the spatula down. He approaches, looming over me.

Jace is tall. He puts NBA players to shame. I feel his presence even without looking up and seeing him.

"Look at me, Olivia."

It takes all of my strength to glance up, just a little.

"While I hope that you will be able to get pregnant, I'm not an unreasonable man. I understand that it takes time, and I won't fault you at any point. The apartment is because I want to make sure you have a roof over your head. You don't owe me anything. Okay?"

"Okay."

He seems too good to be true.

Too kind.

Too unrealistic.

I stare into his green eyes. I want to kiss him. But should I?

9

OLIVIA

Staring up into his gaze, I lean in. I feel hypnotized under his spell. I want to kiss him. Taste his lips. He's handsome, more gorgeous than any other man I've been with, and a hell of a lot richer.

Instead, I take a step back, trying to get away, needing space. I can't let my head drift into the clouds, pretending this is something it isn't.

It's a business transaction. That's it.

I trip over my own feet and spill my coffee all over me and his wood floor.

A shriek emits from my lips, along with a curse.

I don't drop my mug, it's still in my hands, but it splashes the contents everywhere.

Including my white t-shirt.

"Are you okay?" Jace's voice is warm and filled with concern.

I pull the wet t-shirt away from my body, the liquid painfully hot against my skin. It takes everything in my power not to rip my clothes off.

He yanks his t-shirt off and hands me his shirt. "Put this on."

"In front of you?" I squeak.

"Or go into the bathroom. It's not like I haven't seen breasts before."

Well, he hasn't seen my boobs. I'd prefer to keep it that way.

He turns the stove down and grabs a kitchen rag to wipe the floor before hurrying to his room.

While he's out of sight, I yank my shirt off and slip his t-shirt on. It's warm and smells uniquely of Jace. It's a musky scent, earthy and clean. I try not to take a huge whiff, but the smell surrounds me, and I honestly don't mind it.

I like his pheromones, or it's been too long since I've had sex.

Probably both.

———

After breakfast, I get dressed, and Jace hands me the keys.

Matteo dropped them off while I was in the bathroom getting ready.

Jace scribbles down the address of the apartment. "Do you need directions?"

"I can look up the place on my phone," I say. I don't want to inconvenience him any more than I already have. Doesn't he need to be at work? He has a huge company to run, and I'm getting in the way, keeping him from doing his job.

"Okay. I'll be in touch with the paperwork, doctor's appointments, and anything else you need. Matteo works for me, and if you can't reach me for some reason and it's an emergency, you can always contact him."

He jots down Matteo's phone number.

I'm not sure what type of emergency I'd have, but I smile and nod, trying to show my appreciation.

"Thank you," I say.

Jace walks me out, opening the wrought-iron gates so that I can leave. "This place is practically a fortress," I say.

"That's the point."

I pull out my car keys and unlock the front door, opening it. I suppose the security is because he's a billionaire, but I refrain from mentioning it. There's no point in reminding the man that he could bathe in a tub of money.

Does he worry that he could be held for ransom or his home burglarized because he has enough money to buy the entire state of California if it were for sale?

I'm surprised he doesn't own a chain of islands. Someplace quiet and remote.

Maybe he does, and I just don't know about it? It's not like he's telling me his secrets, revealing himself to me. He doesn't have to. I work for him, not the other way around.

Jace stands just a few feet away, watching as I climb into my car. He folds his arms across his chest. His eyes tighten, and he shakes his head, coming around to the driver's side.

Did I forget something?

He leans down just as I start the engine.

I roll down my window while reaching for my phone to input the address into GPS.

Jace glances at the dashboard. "Do you have enough gas to get you to the apartment?"

I don't know how far a drive it is to where I'm going yet. "Let me see," I say and punch in the address that he gave me.

It's a few miles, with traffic twenty-five minutes is what GPS estimates on the screen. I have less than an eighth of a tank. The empty tank indicator light hasn't come on yet.

I should make it to the apartment, but anywhere else will be tough until payday.

Jace reaches in through the open window and hands me a crisp one-hundred-dollar bill.

I didn't even see him reach into his wallet. I was too busy punching in the address of the apartment he was sending me to.

"Take it," Jace says, offering me the money that I asked for last night to cover gas for the car.

"Only if it comes out of my pay." I oblige and retrieve the bill from his fingers, slipping it into my wallet. While I'm not looking for a handout, I am relieved he's willing to help by giving me an advance.

He cocks a sideways grin. "Don't worry. The contract will all be laid out, including a payment schedule, expectations, and contractual requirements. I'll come by this evening to your apartment with the paperwork," Jace says.

He makes it sound quite overwhelming. "Do I need a lawyer?" I ask. It's not like I have the money for one, but I don't want to get in over my head again. I'm still paying the price for the last mistake that I made, marrying John.

I thought I needed him in my life to help me raise my son, but all he did was make things worse.

Much worse.

"I will go over everything thoroughly with you, but if you want to bring a lawyer, I won't stop you. I'll swing by this evening when I get off work. I'll call you when I'm on my way."

"All right," I say. There's no way I can afford a lawyer.

He steps away from my car, and I manually roll up the window with the crank. There's nothing fancy about my vehicle. It was a bottom-of-the-line model, the cheapest I could get my hands on and afford.

———

After I fill up my gas tank and tuck the remainder of the money back into my purse, I head straight to the apartment.

I'm not sure what to expect. I follow the directions and parallel park out on the street. There's a parking garage, but I don't have a vehicle pass to get inside.

I grab my duffel bag of clothes and sling my purse over my shoulder as I step out of the car. I lock the car doors and use the key Jace gave me to enter through the main entrance.

I head up to the elevator. I glance at the apartment number scribbled in Jace's handwriting. I ride the elevator up to the fourth floor and then step out, glancing around for 4B.

The hallway is well lit. The building smells of new construction, like fresh paint. It appears well maintained from the interior of the hallway.

I find my apartment quickly enough and shove my key into the lock, opening the door. I flip on the light, surprised by the magnitude of the apartment.

It's huge and bigger than my place. The walls smell of fresh paint and look pristine. Morning light streams in through the open curtains, making the apartment bright and sunny. The walls are a warm yellow, not blinding, but soft and vibrant.

He just happened to have an extra apartment available.

I shouldn't ask questions, but the rent for this place must be a fortune. Why does he have an apartment just lying around?

Was it for his mistress?

No, it's not like he's married.

It seems too good to be true.

My phone buzzes, startling me. I pull it out of my purse and glance at the screen. There's a message from Jace and a missed call from Harper.

Why is my stomach bubbly and in knots with Jace's message? It's like I'm in high school all over again.

So, what do you think?

I assume he's asking me about the apartment. But I might as well make him spell it out.

About...

He answers me right away.

The apartment. Is it okay?

I just walked in the door. I haven't even had time to explore it, but the place is fully furnished and gorgeous. I'm in love.

With the apartment.

It'll do.

He doesn't answer me. There aren't even three dots to indicate that he's texting me back.

Did I just insult him?

I drop my bag by the front door, slip out of my shoes, and examine the place thoroughly. Since no one is here to give me a tour, I do it myself.

The apartment is a two-bedroom with more than enough space. It's twice the size of my last place, and I'm sure the rent is four or five times more than what I was paying.

I head into the kitchen for a glass of water. I open the cabinet, and the place is fully stocked with dishware. I'm not surprised. The rest of the apartment is furnished.

Out of curiosity, I open the fridge. I don't expect to find anything. There are a few bottles of water, some condiments in the door, but nothing perishable.

I run the tap and pour myself a glass of water. I know it's not a hotel, and I won't be charged ten dollars a bottle for water, but I don't want to take what isn't mine.

This isn't my home.

It's temporary housing until I get myself situated or pregnant.

I grab a seat at the kitchen table and listen to Harper's message, telling me how great she's doing, how she's pregnant, and that she misses me and to give her a call.

I want to call her, but what do I say? How do I explain this arrangement without sounding crazy? I dial her number but don't hit send. She's my best friend, but would she understand? I hadn't told her that I was homeless. While she knows about John and Austin, she doesn't know about Luka and the mafia.

It's better if I don't say anything. Worrying her won't do either of us any good.

Maybe it's best kept a secret.

And I don't want to take advantage of the situation or of Jace. He's being nice, and while it's because he wants me to be the surrogate for his baby, I have to tread carefully.

I text Jace one simple word.

Thanks.

He starts typing, and I'm holding my breath, waiting for his response to come through.

Whatever he typed, he must have erased the message, because the three blinking dots vanish.

10

JACE

"You are way out of her league," Matteo says as he corners me. The minute I get into the office, he's on me.

I shove my phone into my pocket. I've been texting Olivia, but I need to stop. She's a distraction I can't have. No one can know that I'm in the process of hiring a surrogate. Eventually, the news will come out, but I want it to be on my terms when I'm ready for the media to press me with dozens of questions.

I kept Matteo under control at the house when he dropped off the apartment keys. But it's not like I can keep secrets from him.

"Who?" I try to play him off like I don't know who or what he's talking about.

I brush past him for my office, but he's on my heels, following me and shutting the door behind himself.

"Don't fuck around, Jace. The girl, the surrogate. You could do so much better if you just settled down with a wife."

I scoff at his suggestion. "That's not happening. Olivia is just going to be the surrogate. Nothing else." I know to keep my dick in check. Although sometimes the damn thing has a mind of its own.

"Right." Matteo snorts.

He doesn't believe me. And why should he? I've slept with half the women in the city. Well, probably not half, but sometimes it feels that way when I constantly run into them.

"Listen, she's down on her luck right now. She's willing to help me out, and I'm willing to extend a hand and give her a place to stay."

"You could have just hired her as your assistant."

"Now there's an idea," I say and stare at him. "Hire her and fire you."

Matteo rolls his eyes. "Nice joke there, boss."

He's not the least bit worried about his job or me kicking his ass to the curb. And for a good reason, he's got job security as second to the don unless he crosses me.

Anyone who crosses me ends up dead.

But he would never betray me, unlike my sister Maia.

"Sit," I command.

"I'm not one of your soldiers, Jace. You can't order me around," Maia says. She folds her arms defensively across her chest as she stands opposite my desk.

"I can if you're living under my roof," I say, reminding her who is in charge. "It's time for you to settle down, and Ryder is one of the finest men I work with and a capo. He will take care of you."

Maia rolls her eyes at me. "I don't need taking care of. I'm not some girl you can just marry off for two goats and an ox."

"This is what our father would have wanted," I say. I inherited his position, his property, and his men. I also have the serious task of looking after Maia, ensuring she's

protected, which isn't easy considering her love of running away from home.

A man like Ryder would tame and protect her. It's what she needs to survive in this cold, cruel world.

"What about what I want?" Maia steps around my desk.

I placate her. "What do you want?"

"My freedom. Father might have left you everything, but I'm his heir, too. I should have a piece of the money."

"There is no money," I scoff at her suggestion. "Father was broke, and I supported his endeavors. Barone Industries kept him afloat. It's why he changed his will to leave me everything."

"I don't believe you!"

I remain calm and collected. There's no sense in arguing with her. "What do you need the money for?" I ask.

I'm not a selfish man. I take care of my family. Since my father's death, I've turned the mafia family around, bringing in more money to launder, and have given all my men a pay raise.

"To get away from you, Jace." She stares down at me. The girl isn't cut out for blood. She'd be safer, sent away, forced to live far from Los Angeles.

But there are other mafia families across the country. Any number of them could seize on the opportunity to take her, abduct, and torture her to get to me.

"You're a murderer!" Maia's nostrils flare with the accusation. "And a monster! How many men have you killed, Jace? Papa would be ashamed by the bloodshed, the deaths piling up."

I'm silent, considering my options. Maia is a loose end, and an unraveled thread that, if pulled on, could destroy everything.

She must be stopped.

My silence must be aggravating to her. Her accusations grow even wilder. "Did you murder Papa too?"

"That's enough!" I bellow and reach for her shirt, grabbing her by the lapels, pulling her close.

The middle button on her blouse pops, and it reveals a wire.

Who the hell is she working for?

The Feds?

"I was feeling generous, offering Olivia a place to stay," I say.

I don't need to admit there's a selfish part of me also making sure that she doesn't betray me. I have surveillance in the halls, on the building, and will know if she has any visitors who are trouble.

"Can we drop the subject?" I'm not asking. I'm telling him it's done and that we need to move on to other matters.

"Fine. What do you need me to do?" Matteo asks.

"Contact the surrogacy agency and let them know that we're going in another direction."

"You don't want to wait until after you've signed the paperwork? The lawyer called the office this morning and will have the papers ready by four this afternoon."

"Good." I breathe a sigh of relief.

"Are you sure about this?" Matteo asks.

"Hiring a surrogate or Olivia?" I suspect he has reservations about how I've handled this arrangement, and I don't blame him. It's not the least bit typical. But since when do I ever do anything by the books?

From the beginning, I made it clear to him that I wanted a girl who I could get to know in person, not on paper. Honesty and integrity are shown and not something that can be jotted down like accolades on a resume.

"It's the girl."

I sit at my desk. "Do you have something on her?" I expect that he's run a background check on her behind my back.

He's looking out for me and for what's in my best interest.

"She has some pretty staggering medical bills," Matteo says.

He doesn't elaborate, and I don't ask.

"Anyone without medical insurance can easily become broke," I say. It's the system. I've seen it countless times.

Honestly, I don't want to know if he found anything else.

Unless she wants to tell me, I don't need to go digging for dirt. Everyone has baggage. I have enough skeletons in the closet.

Her past is none of my business.

As long as she's healthy and the doctor agrees that she is a good candidate for surrogacy, whatever debts she has are in the past.

The money she earns from me will help pay them off.

Matteo shuts his mouth.

He's wise to steer the conversation away from whatever he found. "I just worry Olivia might be taking advantage of you."

I laugh at the absurdity of his suggestion. "I made her the offer. It wasn't the other way around," I remind him. She had no clue the offer was coming.

Matteo is getting under my skin.

"And I'm telling you I'm against it, but you're going to do what you think is best."

"Why are you so against it?" I ask. The obvious answer would be the potential for a lawsuit. But that's the least of my concerns.

She's not looking for a payday or a handout. Olivia needs help.

"The girl wreaks of trouble," Matteo says.

Tell me something I don't know.

I refrain from mentioning that she's been living in her car. It's not fair to Olivia to divulge her secret. But I'm sure Matteo has the cogs turning in his head, wondering why I'm letting her stay at one of our properties.

"Trouble isn't a crime," I say.

Besides, it's not like we follow the law.

There's a world that many don't know about, the underworld, and I control it.

Being a mafia boss has its perks. My day job offers a front for money laundering and contacts for many of our illegal enterprises.

"Getting too close to the surrogate could bring trouble," Matteo says. "She could go digging into your past."

She doesn't have the resources to find out the truth. If the Feds can't pin me for murder, then I'm not worried about this girl getting me locked up.

I roll my eyes. "When did you become soft?"

His gaze hardens.

I've insulted him.

I'm done talking about Olivia. "You're dismissed," I say and gesture for him to leave my office. "Shut the door on your way out."

"Yes, sir." He retreats out of the office, closing the door behind himself.

———

The lawyer brings the paperwork, and I text Olivia that we're on the way over with the papers.

Within the hour, we're sitting at her kitchen table going over the contract, the requirements, the fact that after the first trimester, she'll be living at my place.

The signing takes quite a while, but Olivia doesn't have any objections to any of it. She asks a few questions and then signs and initials all the places that are required.

I sign the documents as well before walking the lawyer to the door and bidding goodbye.

"Are you going?" Olivia asks. "I mean, you don't have to. I haven't had dinner yet."

"Have you gone shopping for food?" I know the fridge is empty. No one's been living in the apartment that I gave her for quite some time. A cousin of mine lived there previously for a few months while in town, but he returned to Italy.

"I picked up a few things at the market across the street, but I haven't done any major grocery shopping."

Well, it's not like one hundred dollars is going to get her far at the grocery store when I gave her that money for gas for her car, too.

I pull out my wallet.

"What are you doing?"

"How much do you have in your bank account?" I ask. I can't imagine it's much. I could have Matteo find out the exact number, but that isn't how I work. I expect honesty.

She laughs nervously. "You don't ask someone that question."

"I'm guessing not much since you were living in your car and your gas tank was practically on empty this morning." I pull out another hundred-dollar bill. "I want you to eat healthy while you're trying to get pregnant."

"I know. I read the contract. No alcohol. No drugs. No fun." Olivia smirks, but I get the notion that she's teasing me. "I promise I will take good care of your little bun in my oven."

Her words make my heart strum.

I exhale a sharp breath and steer the conversation back to business.

"I will wire the advance to your account today, but you should have cash on you. The market across the street is cash only, and they have the freshest fruits and vegetables. They cost more, but they're organic, and I want the absolute best for my baby."

"Of course," Olivia says. There's a faint smile on her face, like she's pleased to do this for me.

She doesn't mock me. She's calm and collected.

"What do you want to do about dinner? Take out doesn't seem healthy," she asks.

It's already late, and going down to the store, even just across the street, will take time, as will cooking dinner.

"Well, you're not pregnant yet. I think if we order food in and have it delivered, it will be fine for tonight," I say.

I'm glad she's taking my requests seriously, all of them.

"Okay. I don't know what's available on this side of town. Do you know who delivers?" she asks.

The familiar places that I order from are a bit far from the apartment. I pull out my phone and check the local listings. "There's Chinese, Thai, Italian, Japanese. The list goes on," I say. "What do you have a taste for?"

She licks her lips.

The motion makes my cock stir.

Down, boy. She cannot be eliciting that type of response. I need to keep myself in check.

"Everything sounds delicious. I should have eaten more than a salad for lunch," Olivia says with a nervous laugh. "Now I'm starving."

Me too, but my desire is less about food and more about her.

11

OLIVIA

Jace orders us Italian for dinner, and I pull dishes from the cabinet when the food arrives.

"Have you thought about what you're going to do after the baby is born?" Jace asks.

I'm not sure what he means. I'll be giving up the baby. There isn't much to think about.

He must see the frown on my face.

"What do you want to do for a career?" Jace asks.

"Oh, I'm not sure," I say. I sit at the table and nurse my water. I wish it were a tall glass of wine.

"Dream job?" He opens the lids on each of the dishes and then serves me along with himself.

"I used to paint."

"You're an artist," Jace says and smiles. "I can see that."

"Starving artist?" I laugh and reach for my water, taking a sip.

He's kind enough not to comment. "Do you have any of your artwork around?" Jace glances around the apartment.

The walls are mostly bare. Not that I've had time to put any of my artwork up, even if I had it handy.

"Uh, no." I shove a forkful of pasta into my mouth, so I don't have to elaborate.

I'm not sure whether he notices or not, but his gaze is on me for far too long.

"I'd love to see some of your art. Is it for sale?" Jace asks.

"Most of it was destroyed in a fire," I say.

He nods like he's putting the pieces together. Why I was living in my car. Again, he's polite enough not to keep forcing the issue. "I don't know anyone at the local art gallery, but I can make a few phone calls, only if you want my help. I don't want to overstep," he says.

He's sweet, a little too helpful. And while I appreciate his kindness, I also can't accept it.

"No, that's all right. I'm sure I'd just disappoint them when I end up pregnant in a few months and leave my job."

Jace takes another bite of pasta.

The room is quiet. Too quiet.

You can hear a pin drop.

I should have turned the television on for background noise. Anything to avoid the awkwardness. Why am I so bad at relationships? Is it because of what happened?

Was I always this much of a mess?

"Why would you quit?" Jace asks.

"Oh, I just assumed that you'd want me off my feet and at home. You said I'd be living with you after I'm pregnant."

"I'm sure you'll want to take time off when you get closer to your delivery date, but there's no reason that you can't work as long as you and the baby are healthy. Unless you just don't want to work?"

Is he judging me?

"No, I came into your office yesterday looking for employment," I say, reminding him how we met. The exact reason he doesn't need—because of Luka Caruso.

He can never find out the truth.

I didn't plan to become a surrogate. That's for sure. But I did love my time while pregnant, carrying my son. And the money he's offering would get rid of my problems with the Carusos and get me back on my feet.

"How about I get you a position with my company?" Jace asks.

"Won't that complicate things?" I can't tell him about Luka.

Will he expect company secrets if I work for the elusive billionaire? Or did Luka want me to carry Jace's child?

My head hurts just thinking about it, and I can't ask Luka, nor would I want to.

"It's probably not ideal," he says.

At least he's being honest. It makes one of us. But I can't tell him about Luka, not without putting his life in danger. As well as my own.

"But we are both adults and can be professional. And I'd know and approve of your maternity leave without any issue," Jace says with a grin. It's like he's talking himself into hiring me.

I laugh under my breath. "Well, when you put it like that, how can I say no?" If Luka gets wind of the job offer and me turning it down, it won't end well. But how would he know?

Unless one of his men works for Jace; the mafia is everywhere, and I can't trust anyone.

"When do I start?" I ask.

I finish the last bite of my dinner and start to pack the leftovers and put the contents into the refrigerator. I don't want to waste any food.

Jace stands and helps me clean up the dishes, taking them to the sink to wash. "First thing Monday morning. You can say no if you don't want to work for me. I swear I won't hold it against you."

He's giving me an out, but I can't take it. I do need the money, and while an advance is nice, he's not going to start paying me until I'm pregnant. I can't expect him to keep handing me money whenever I need something.

It'll be months until I'm pregnant, carrying his child, assuming I can conceive again.

"Would you be my boss?" I ask. I shut the fridge and come over to the sink to start on the dishes, but he's already plugged the sink, running hot water and filling it with suds.

"I'm technically everyone's boss," Jace says, "but if you're concerned, I can assign you to work in a department that I don't deal with on a daily basis."

Given my lack of experience, I'm not sure what Jace would have me do, but I don't care. Getting a paycheck of my own for working would be satisfying. It would also help with my debts.

"I'm not worried. Are you? I mean, you'd have to see me every day, and I could be carrying your son or daughter." I want to know what he's thinking and if he can maintain professionalism in the workplace.

Because what he's suggesting is insane.

But is it any crazier than me being a surrogate for him?

12

EIGHT MONTHS LATER

OLIVIA

I can't believe it. I'm pregnant. I mean, sure, I was trying to conceive, and after fertility treatments, it gave me the best odds, but I didn't think it would happen.

My fear had gotten the best of me. Wondering if Jace would hate me for not being able to conceive, sue me for the advance of funds, and force me to pay back all the expenses from living in the apartment he's provided.

It's not like I've been sitting around all day doing nothing. I've been working full time for Jace's company, Barone Industries, running the reception desk for the fifteenth floor. It pays well and keeps me busy. Plus, I like not having to go to Jace for money. I mean, he still technically pays me, but I'm earning that money fair and square.

Asking for an advance was humiliating.

I don't ever want to do that again, which encouraged me to go for it. Why wouldn't I take it if he was willing to extend a hand and give me a job?

At least I can save up money because I'll have to find somewhere else to live after the baby is born. But Jace is also paying me handsomely for my time while pregnant, so I should be able to afford a place of my own.

That's months away.

I stare at the pregnancy test. All six that I took show that I'm pregnant. I didn't believe the first one and thought it might have been a false positive.

But every test is showing positive, and they're different brands.

It can't be a fluke.

I'm pregnant.

My stomach bubbles with nerves. I should text Jace, but I'm heading to work this morning. Telling him in person, that feels like the right thing to do.

He'll be happy.

Ecstatic.

I want to see that look of joy on his face.

I shower, dress, and head into the office.

Hurrying toward his office, the door is open, but the lights are off.

Jace isn't in yet.

He usually is in before I show up and he stays well after I leave. The man practically lives in the office.

How he plans to raise a kid is beyond me.

Where is he?

Is everything okay?

"Looking for someone?" Matteo asks. He holds a cup of coffee in his hand, and the steam wafts into the air before he takes a sip.

"I wanted to speak with Mr. Barone," I say, careful not to call him by his first name. We're casual when we're together, but at work, he's the boss. I have to make sure that I keep it professional. I don't want rumors flying, especially when people find out that I'm pregnant.

I don't intend to tell anyone that I'm the surrogate for his baby. If he decides to tell people, that's on him.

"He's busy this morning," Matteo says. His tone is curt. He doesn't like me.

He's never liked me since the moment I showed up for my interview.

Does he know Luka Caruso? Do they work together in secret?

No, if that were the case, he'd have convinced Jace to hire me. And I get the feeling he isn't on my team at all.

Does he know about the surrogacy arrangement?

"Thanks," I say. I consider asking Matteo to let Jace know that I stopped by, but that would only arouse further suspicion. It's best if I text Jace myself.

I pull out my phone and head back to my desk. I want to grab a cup of coffee, but I had promised Jace that I would give up caffeine, especially coffee, the moment I found out I was pregnant.

That damn contract!

Decaf doesn't seem worth the hassle, plus it still has a minute amount of caffeine. I slump into my desk chair and fumble with my phone.

I search through my contacts and find Jace. I text him a quick message.

Can we meet up tonight?

It feels like torture waiting for him to respond. I'm not a patient person. My foot taps nervously against the floor.

I can't tell whether he's read the message or not. But he hasn't responded or attempted to answer—no three blinking dots.

It's silent.

I put my phone down on my desk and boot up the computer. I have work to do, and when he comes into the office, he'll have to step off the elevator, at which point I'll see him. Assuming he doesn't respond to my text first.

Jace doesn't come into the office.

He doesn't answer my text.

I know I shouldn't be worried. Maybe he's out of town on business. It's not like I'm his keeper. He doesn't have to tell me his schedule. I'm not his girlfriend or wife.

But I would appreciate it if he answered his text message. Even if he's out of town, he could still respond.

Matteo rushes past my desk for the elevator in quite a hurry. He repeatedly taps the down button of the elevator in haste.

"You know, that doesn't make the elevator car come any quicker," I say.

He shoots me a look. It's the same look of disbelief that I've seen on Jace once or twice. Except with Jace, it's not laced with annoyance.

Matteo storms over to my desk. "I don't know what game you're playing, but Jace will never want to be with you. Ever."

What is he talking about?

"Excuse me?" I cough, embarrassed by his suggestion.

Has he lost his mind? Jace and I aren't anything more than professionals. We haven't spent much time together since the initial contract was signed.

Jace checks in on me, brings me healthy snacks, occasionally takes me out to lunch, but we're colleagues at work. Maybe the snack part is a little unusual, but I'm also trying to get pregnant, and he's made it known that he wants me to eat healthy.

The elevator dings, and I've never been so relieved to watch someone step inside and the doors shut behind them.

What the hell was that about?

Did Jace tell him something about me?

I grab a bottle of water and take a swig—my heart pitter-patters in my chest when my cell phone lights up with a text message.

Swing by my place after work. We need to talk.

13

JACE

There's a firm knock on the front door.

"You've really downgraded your residence," Matteo says, glancing around the empty apartment.

He knows this isn't my place.

Well, I own the entire building, but I don't live here.

This apartment was supposed to be empty. Security alerted me this morning that the apartment had a squatter.

At least that's what I'd been told. But it wasn't just a random homeless person living in the apartment.

"Isn't your girlfriend living in this building?" Matteo asks.

"She's not my girlfriend," I say, correcting him. I clear my throat. "Yes, Olivia is living next door. It looks like one of Caruso's men was watching her."

There's surveillance equipment hooked up inside the apartment, revealing several rooms, including Olivia's bedroom and the bathroom.

"Or it could just be a pervert," Matteo says.

No one knows my connection with Olivia, but I still can't help but suspect it's the Caruso family behind this invasion of privacy.

"Whoever it is, they haven't come back all day," I say. I've been waiting for them, with my gun, prepared for a fierce interrogation.

"The surveillance is pretty low tech," Matteo says. "Caruso would plant bugs and wouldn't have his buddies next door. It reminds me more of a really bad sting by some lame-ass cops."

I don't believe that she's been talking to the police or anyone else. Olivia doesn't know anything, least of all that I'm mafia.

And she can never find out.

"I hope you're right." I want it to be a pervert whom I can pound the shit out of and know without a doubt that she's safe. "Either way, I can't let her stay in the apartment complex any longer."

I don't feel safe letting her live here.

"What do you intend to do?" Matteo asks. "Move her to another building?"

"I've already texted her to meet me at my place."

Memories of her spending the night months ago flood through my mind. Images of her wearing only one of my t-shirts stirs my cock. I clear my throat and turn away from Matteo, wandering around the apartment one last time.

I need a moment to compose myself, and there's plenty of surveillance equipment and evidence left behind to investigate.

Matteo glances over at a table opposite where I stand. "Did you see these markings?" He points to the writing in Russian. "Could it be the Bratva?"

The Russians are unpredictable. They're violent. That's not to say that we aren't, but we don't murder cops or judges.

My family is bound by a code of honor, Omerta. We don't kill unless it's necessary. I don't find enjoyment in bloodying my hands, but I do what I must.

"I hope not," I mutter. We have a relationship with them and understand that we don't mix in each other's businesses. "This doesn't seem like a Bratva operation."

The Russians don't sit around and watch an innocent woman. They're not known for their patience.

If they wanted something from Olivia, they'd have snatched her, interrogated her, and then murdered her when they were done with her.

Another reason I want her out of the apartment complex. She's not safe here.

"You're right. It's too clean. There'd be blood all over the walls and floor if this were their mess," Matteo says.

Is he trying to make light of the situation? I don't find his humor particularly funny.

I shoot him a look, and he merely shrugs. "What?" Matteo asks. "You don't agree?"

"Call in one of our soldiers. I want to know without a doubt who was keeping tabs on Olivia and why," I say. "Have them bring whoever it is in for questioning."

I intend to sit in on the interrogation when it's time.

————

Returning home, I make sure to pick up a few extra groceries on my way back and put everything away in the refrigerator.

There are barely two minutes to spare before I hear a car door slam outside.

It's distant, barely audible, but I'm on high alert after today.

I glance out the window.

Olivia is approaching the gate, which is locked.

A few seconds later, my phone buzzes with a text message from her.

I'm here.

This time I don't go outside. I grab the remote and unlock the wrought-iron gate, allowing Olivia entrance inside the property.

Once I'm satisfied that she's inside the gate and no one follows her, I hit the button and begin to close the gate. It does have the ability to close on its own, but I don't want to allow anyone the opportunity inside my property who doesn't belong.

Especially since someone seems to be watching Olivia.

Is it because she works for me?

Whoever has been spying on her, do they think we're in a relationship? Have they been waiting for me to show up for scandalous photos?

Well, there aren't any.

There isn't anything worthy of blackmail material.

I've been careful. I always have to be cautious around people, no matter where I am. Anyone could be recording what I say, watching what I do, and trying to entrap me.

I unlock the front door just as Olivia steps up onto the porch. I yank open the door, trying to appear casual about it, but my heart is jack hammering in my chest.

Why does she make me feel like this? Is it because she's a woman and I'm a man?

Is it as simple as biology?

"Come inside," I say and step aside to let her into the house.

"Thanks."

She slips out of her shoes, leaving them at the front entrance. Olivia is far more relaxed than the last time she was in my home. That was months ago. It feels like a lifetime has passed. I keep waiting for the good news, hoping that she'll tell me she's pregnant, but I know it takes time.

She had to go in for medical tests, injections, procedures, and then we wait.

The waiting is excruciating.

Agonizing.

I'm not the most patient man. And the fact I want this more than almost anything in the world makes it even more painful.

I want a son to follow in my footsteps.

"I was just about to put on dinner. I assume you haven't eaten yet?" I ask.

Wordlessly, Olivia shakes her head. There's a faint smile on her lips. "Not yet."

"It's still early," I say.

She must have just gotten off work and come straight here from the office. She's dressed in a black pencil skirt and dark red blouse that hugs her breasts.

I try not to stare.

I always try to maintain professionalism with all of my employees. But she's the only one trying to get pregnant with my child.

Maybe it is biology to blame, the fact that while I'm not sleeping with her, my seed is still planted in her womb. Just being in her proximity, I have to take a step back.

I want to back her up against the wall, push her skirt up, and rip her panties free. Then I'd bury my cock deep inside her.

The room is sweltering.

I head for the thermostat and adjust the temperature, cooling it down a degree.

"Come in, make yourself at home," I say as I lead her into the kitchen.

"What's for dinner?" she asks.

There's an innocence about her.

Olivia is young, far younger than most of the women I've slept with recently. Just imagining her naked feels like I'm robbing the cradle, but she's well over eighteen. Hell, she's old enough to drink legally.

"Filet mignon, green beans, with couscous and a side of salad." I've already figured out the menu for this evening. I had to pick up all the ingredients at the grocery store before returning home.

Her tongue darts out and swipes across her top lip. "It all sounds delicious."

I stare at her.

Fuck.

She looks delicious.

Inwardly, I groan and clear my throat. I cannot have feelings for her. If I act on it, the surrogacy will have to end. The past eight months would be wasted, all for a little piece of ass.

I don't do relationships. I have an aversion to them, so fucking her once for a good time seems like an even bigger waste.

I'd hate myself tomorrow.

I grab the steak from the fridge and unwrap it from the butcher's paper, placing it on a plate to season.

"How did you learn to cook?" Olivia asks. She approaches the sink and washes her hands.

Does she plan on helping?

"My father taught me," I say. "He loved grilling anything and everything imaginable. Some of his concoctions were wonderful, but a few were downright dreadful."

Olivia chuckles under her breath. "Like what?"

"Fruit salad, for instance, is not great on the grill. Sure, you can grill up a few pineapples to top on your meat, but an entire fruit salad grilled in a foil bag was not a favorite."

She purses her lips, probably imagining the sight. "I don't know. I love cooked blueberries, especially in muffins or pancakes."

"Sure, when they're baked, but he'd have tried putting pancakes on the grill and then been shocked when the liquid just oozed down the grates."

Olivia bursts out laughing. "You have to be joking."

"Am I?" I ask with a laugh. "I wish I were teasing. What about you? Do you cook often?" I can't imagine she can afford to eat out all the time.

"Not often, but I do like to bake," Olivia says and pins me with her gaze. "Right now, I have a bun in the oven."

My mouth is dry as I stare at her.

"You're pregnant?"

Is she serious?

A huge grin spreads across her face. "Surprise!" Olivia giggles and nods excitedly. "I made a doctor's appointment for next week, but I peed on six pregnancy tests, and they all came back positive."

I want to throw my arms around her, pull her against me, and embrace her in a hug. "Can I give you a hug?" I ask.

I want to celebrate, but I don't want to make her uncomfortable, either. It's a fine line, and the fact I'm currently her boss doesn't help matters. But I swore that I'd be okay with it, that hiring her would be good for her and the company.

"Yes," she says and steps closer.

The grin she wears makes my heart soar. I pull her tight and have to refrain from lifting her off the ground and spinning her around. She's not a child.

"I want you to move in here with me immediately."

"What? I thought we were waiting until after the first trimester?" Olivia asks. She pulls back, her brow knitted, and untangles from my embrace. "The contract stated that—"

I interrupt her. "I received a phone call earlier today. I'm not sure how to say this gently, but someone's been keeping tabs on you."

"What?" She steps farther away from me. Like I've burned her. Olivia folds her arms across her chest. "I don't understand."

"I have one of my colleagues keeping an eye out for when the suspect reemerges," I say, leaving out the part where I intend to interrogate and torture him myself. I will get to the bottom of this and find out what he's doing watching Olivia.

Her voice cracks. "You don't know who it is?"

I shake my head. There's no sense in worrying her with the number of enemies that I've made. The list is long.

"We will find out, but you're pregnant. And we discussed you are staying after your first trimester. It'll just be a little sooner," I say.

I open the fridge, pulling out the green beans. I wash them under running water before cutting off the ends.

"Won't you get sick of me?" Olivia asks.

"Your safety is my number one priority. Yours and that baby you're carrying," I remind her.

"What about my stuff?" Olivia runs a hand through her hair.

"I'll go with you back to your apartment to grab your things and bring you back here." My answer is firm.

I have to protect my child that she's carrying as much as I feel the need to look after her.

She emits a soft sigh. I don't want to fight with her. Is she giving in?

"I'm not going to be able to convince you otherwise, am I?" she asks.

"No, once I make up my mind, it's done."

I grab a pot from the cabinet below and the steamer basket, filling it with water, preparing to put it on the stove.

Olivia opens the cabinets, unfamiliar with my house. "What are you looking for?" I ask.

"I was going to help with setting the table, but I realize that I don't know where anything is located."

"Just sit and relax," I say. "I've got dinner. You can help clean up if you want to do something."

She scrunches her nose at my suggestion. "I hate doing the dishes."

"Me too," I say, laughing under my breath. "And here I thought you moving in would be doing me a favor."

Olivia rolls her eyes, smiling at my brand of humor. At least she's not upset with my suggestion and making her move in. I thought I'd have to fight her and convince her that it wasn't safe, even showing her the apartment next door and the surveillance equipment we found.

I'm glad I won't have to do that. Seeing and knowing are two different things.

I don't want to put her through that invasion of privacy.

She grabs a seat at the counter on one of the stools. "Are you going to tell me why you're still single? You're hot, rich as fuck, and according to the papers, unattached."

Hiding the smile on my face, I glance up at her. I've never seen this side of her, vulgar, honest, open.

"Don't believe everything you read," I say.

Does she think I'm hot?

I find her attractive. It's hard not to with her sinful hip sway. Every time she walks and is in front of me, my gaze lands right on her perfectly proportioned ass.

But I can't act on those impulses. Even if I wanted to, it could ruin everything.

And now that she's pregnant, there's too much at stake.

14

OLIVIA

Jace accompanies me back to the apartment to gather my belongings. There isn't much that's mine, just the clothes I've accumulated over the past couple of months. I grab my bag and toss my clothes inside, everything that I own.

Most of the items in the apartment aren't mine. I didn't decorate. There aren't any pictures hanging, and I didn't have the supplies to do any artwork of my own.

I zip up my bag and head to the kitchen. On the counter is my phone charger. I grab the cord, shoving it into the front zipper of the duffel bag.

"What about the food in the fridge?" I ask, pointing at the full refrigerator. I just went shopping last week.

Maybe it doesn't matter to Jace, but I don't want to waste perfectly good food.

"I'll send Matteo to swing by, and he can clean out your fridge, clean up the place."

That wasn't quite what I meant, but if it's not going to waste, then it'll suffice.

I'm afraid to ask if he knows who exactly was watching the apartment, eavesdropping.

Was it Caruso or one of his men?

Jace has no idea the connection that I have with them.

They're mafia.

Really bad guys.

They'd kill me if I spoke about them, and asking now, while we could be under surveillance, could get both of us hurt, or worse.

I have to tread carefully. But undoubtedly, if it's Luka Caruso or his men, they won't stop just because I've moved. They'll never stop hunting me down.

Another reason I have to follow through with having Jace's child.

After he pays me, I can pay off my debt to Caruso. Will the money be enough, or will he own me forever? Men like Caruso don't just go away. It doesn't matter that I didn't sign the deal with my blood.

"Come on, let's get out of here," Jace says, leading me to the front door. He holds out his hand, taking my duffel bag from me.

"I can carry that," I say. The bag isn't that heavy. It barely weighs anything. His briefcase for work is probably heavier.

Jace gives a slight shrug. "Just because you can doesn't mean that you should." He opens the door and gestures for me to step out of the apartment.

I lock up the place behind me and hand over the keys. He owns the site. He might as well take back the keys. Besides, if Matteo plans to clean out and empty the fridge, he'll need to gain entrance inside the apartment.

I shuffle down the hallway, glancing at the door beside my apartment.

Is that where the snoop had taken up residence?

I'm afraid to voice my questions aloud.

"Come on," he says again and grabs my elbow, leading me toward the elevator in haste.

It's like he's hiding something, ushering me out of here quickly.

Why? What don't I know? What isn't he telling me?

The moment the elevator doors shut, I fold my arms across my chest. "What's going on, Jace?"

He holds up a hand, indicating to give him a moment.

I roll my eyes, and after we reach the ground floor and step outside, I'm still awaiting his answer. "Are you avoiding me or worried someone might overhear us?" I ask.

"In my profession, I've made quite a few enemies," he says.

I'm not surprised. Was it one of his enemies who has been keeping tabs on me next door? Have they threatened to hurt him? Is that why Jace wasn't at work today?

He opens the trunk and drops my duffel inside before opening the passenger door for me to climb into the vehicle.

Always a gentleman. Even when he's avoiding my questions.

It's hard to imagine him pissing off too many people, but a man with quite a bit of worth, one of the richest in the world, does find himself in the line of fire. At least, I imagine that being the case. I've never found that to be an issue for myself.

"Do you know who was watching me in there?" I ask. Would he tell me if it were Caruso's crew?

"Matteo was keeping an eye on the apartment for a few hours this evening, but he left about an hour ago. We put up our hidden surveillance equipment. If anyone returns, we'll know who it is. But I don't expect much."

"Why is that?" I ask.

Jace pulls out into traffic. The roads are still considerably busy this evening. I try to relax while he drives us farther out of the city and toward his home.

"Oh, we'll catch the guy, but I doubt he'll talk or confess to who he works for," Jace says. His brow tightens, and he reaches for the radio, turning it up to drown out the silence in the vehicle and the discussion between us.

My cell phone buzzes in my pocket, but I don't pull it out and look at it. At least not yet. I don't want questions, and if Luka Caruso is communicating with me, I can't let Jace find out, ever.

It doesn't feel like a one-off incident, but I'm sure Jace knows what he's doing.

Jace is safe. Living with him, I won't have to worry about myself or the child I'm carrying.

He'll protect me.

———

"This is your bedroom," Jace says as he leads me into my new bedroom. He's giving me a tour of his house.

Not that I haven't seen the place before, but it's been months since I've stayed.

And that was only one night.

He carries my duffel bag into the bedroom and places it on the floor beside the dresser. "Do you need help to unpack?" he asks.

"No, I've got it. Thank you," I say. I don't need him to wait on me. I can look after myself. The accommodations are a bonus, and while I enjoyed the apartment that I had been living in, Caruso could find me at any time.

I was alone.

At least now, there's an additional layer of protection with the security system and metal gates.

Jace won't let anything happen to me. If not for my sake, for the child of his that I'm carrying.

"I'll leave you to it. If you need anything, I'm just down the hallway," he says.

Jace steps out of the bedroom and shuts the door behind him.

The minute he's out of the room, I whip out my cell phone and glance at the missed message. I expect one, and there are three, all from the same unfamiliar number.

It has to be Caruso. It's a local number that I don't recognize, and there's no name attached to the caller.

Playing house with your boss.

How does he know that I moved in with Jace?

Is he watching me? Is that who has been watching my apartment? Well, Jace's apartment that I have been living in for the past several months.

I send a quick reply.

Who is this?

Will the mystery caller tell me if it's the Carusos or just continue to threaten and harass me?

What if Jace sees my phone? I have to be careful. I can't let anyone know that I'm dealing with the mafia. The last thing I want is for him to get hurt.

Your payment is late.

Confirmed. It's Luka or one of his goons. It doesn't matter much to me. Whether it's him or a soldier, they all scare me. The fact they have their talons in me is already painful. Anywhere I go in the city, they always find me.

I've done what you asked.

They had insisted that I get hired by Jace Barone. I managed to work for his company. I've been waiting for the day for them to collect.

What will they want? Information? Access? Whatever it is could get me fired, or worse, landed in jail.

We're just getting started.

My stomach sinks. I'm going to vomit. I rush off to the bathroom and flip the lid off the toilet.

Nothing comes up. Maybe I should be grateful, but the pit at the bottom of my stomach sits like an anvil and doesn't go away.

Nausea sweeps over me.

Will it ever end?

I shut off my phone. I don't want to receive another text from Caruso. I'm done with them. I pull out the battery and disconnect my phone. Maybe they know where I live, but they can't reach me.

I won't let them contact me.

If I don't have a phone, then maybe they'll leave me alone.

This place is a fortress. Jace won't let them inside his home, and the gates outside and alarm system should be enough to keep them out.

———

We head into work separately. No one needs to be privy to the fact that I'm living with my boss and having his baby. Surrogate or not, there are rumors that I don't want to get around.

Jace seems to have the same thought on the matter. Besides, our hours aren't necessarily the same. He's the owner, the boss. He can work whenever he wants.

I have set hours to handle the reception desk upstairs.

I grab a cup of coffee and sit at my desk, moving the mouse to wake up the computer.

Jace is already in this morning. The office light was on, but he wasn't in his office when I casually strolled by to get my drink.

I sip the hot liquid. If anyone asks, I'll tell them it's decaf, and by anyone, I mean Jace. No one else knows I'm pregnant. And no one else would care what I'm drinking as long as it's not spiked and affecting my job.

There's a package on my desk, a manilla bubble folder, with something inside. It's addressed to me.

That's highly suspect.

I don't get much mail sent to me, let alone at the office. What I do receive tends to be junk mail, catalogs for picking out office equipment, stuff of that nature.

This doesn't feel like that.

There's no return label.

It's not even stamped. Someone dropped it off.

Who? When? I glance around the office. No one seems to pay me the slightest bit of attention. It is addressed to me. I double-check, wondering if I mistook the label because I'm still half-asleep.

I had trouble falling asleep last night. The bed in Jace's home was comfortable enough, but it felt strange to be under his roof, living with him. Before when I stayed over, the first time, he was a handsome stranger, a man who had made me an offer that, while peculiar, had been in a way quite flattering.

Now, he's my boss.

And while I was excited about working for him, the fact that he is my boss and sleeps down the hallway under the same roof, I'm having trouble wrapping my head around.

I swore we'd keep it professional. Don't get me wrong, we are. We haven't so much as kissed, and while I want to see what he feels like under my body, it can't happen.

It won't happen.

I like my job. Appreciate the fact that I have a roof over my head and a steady paycheck. Sure, the money will start flowing in faster now that I'm carrying his kin, but even so, I don't want to screw this up.

"Hey, stranger," Jace says, stopping over at my desk. He's carrying a giant mug of coffee. It puts mine to shame.

"I hope that's decaf," he says, glancing at my nearly empty cup of coffee.

I don't answer him. Avoiding the statement seems best. "You don't have to worry," I say and give a faint smile. "Everything is going well."

"Good," Jace says and glances down at the package on my desk. "Who is that from?"

But now that he's standing over me, watching me, I can't open the damn envelope. What if it's a message from Caruso?

A lie so easily rattles off my tongue. "It's the information for ordering more toner for the printer," I say.

"Is that contraption out of ink again? I swear we replace it daily."

He's exaggerating, but we do replace the toner quite often. I swear that's how the company makes their money, sending us cartridges practically every week that we need to run the machine.

"It's not that often," I say. "Can I help you with anything?" I glance up at him with eager eyes. I want to send him off so that I can open the envelope. I also don't want anyone getting any ideas about the two of us.

There's nothing to gossip about.

Well, except that I'm carrying his baby.

"Let me take you out to lunch," Jace says.

Is he crazy? We're trying to keep a low profile, not give the rumor mill something to talk about. As much as I want to spend time with Jace outside of work, we can't. We're already living together. I plan on keeping to myself as much as I can, at least for the time being.

"I don't think that's a good idea," I say.

"You'll be home for dinner?" Jace asks, keeping his voice down so that only I can hear his question.

There's nowhere else for me to be. "Yes," I say, staring up into his green eyes. He gives me a thousand-watt grin. "Good. Then it's a date."

"Wait. What?"

Jace turns on his heels and heads back toward his office.

He didn't mean an actual date, I'm sure of it. It's an expression. That's probably what he was referring to, and I'm overreacting.

I rub my forehead and make sure Jace is long gone before I open the envelope. Inside there's a note along with a thumb drive.

You work for us. Turn on your phone, or we'll hurt Jace.

What do they want me to do with the thumb drive? I glance inside the envelope, but there isn't anything else. I toss the envelope into the trash.

The elevator door dings open, and Matteo steps out.

I rest my hand on the desk, burying the thumb drive under my palm. Maybe he won't notice.

"Morning, Olivia," he says. He rarely speaks to me, but today he's decided to be friendly. Wonderful. Is it because of the apartment?

"Morning," I say, forcing a smile.

His brow knits as he studies me in passing. He doesn't approach me, and I'm relieved that he doesn't try to continue the awkward conversation between us. We're not friends. I've barely spoken with the man, ever.

He seems close with Jace, though, and maybe I should get to know him. Then again, if there's any chance that he works with Luka, maybe staying far from him is best.

Once he rounds the corner and is out of sight, I examine the flash drive. It looks ordinary. Without plugging it into a USB slot, there's no way to know if it's empty or there's something on it.

I won't risk plugging it in and installing a virus. I'm not an idiot.

There's no other note. No directions. His threat is real, at least in regard to Jace, but I don't have my phone on me. Is he expecting me to run back to the house, grab it, turn it on, and for me to do whatever he wants?

I shove the flash drive into the desk drawer. I'll deal with Caruso tonight when I get home.

————

Jace heads for the elevator, stopping by my desk on the way to lunch. "Are you sure I can't convince you to come out?"

There's a warm, friendly smile on his face. It's tempting, but I can't accept his offer.

"Thanks, but I'll just grab something quick."

Matteo hurries to catch up with him. "Lunch?" Matteo asks, nodding at Jace.

"Sure."

It looks like he found someone to join him.

My stomach grumbles, and I want to grab lunch, but I wait until he's long gone. I grab my purse and head down the elevator and then outside. I pull my jacket tighter as I hurry down the block for the nearby sandwich joint.

I doubt Jace eats there. He seems like more of a fancy restaurant, five-star, upscale dining kind of guy.

Thankfully, I don't see him when I glance in through the glass windows before opening the door.

"Olivia." Luka's voice startles me from behind.

I see his reflection in the glass as my hand is poised at the entrance of the eatery.

I drop the door handle and spin around to face him.

"Did you get our message?" Luka asks.

I'm surprised to see that he's delivering the message himself. Doesn't he have men who take care of those tasks?

"My phone isn't on me," I say. It's not a lie.

He digs out a burner phone from his pocket, handing it to me.

I purse my lips. How do I get rid of this creep? "I don't want your phone," I say.

"I'm not asking," Luka says. He pushes it into my hand, forcing me to take the device. "We need information, and you're just the perfect person to give it to us. Put the thumb drive into Jace's personal computer, at home."

"What? You're crazy if you think I'm going to do that."

"You will if you want to keep your little lover boy safe."

So, they don't know about the surrogacy arrangement. I almost breathe a sigh of relief. I'm not out of the woods yet. These men are dangerous, and Jace has no idea what he's up against or what I've done, the damage that I could unintentionally inflict.

I refrain from telling Luka that Jace isn't my lover boy. That we're just colleagues. He'll never buy it, and maybe it's better if he thinks we're more than we are. But I'm not sure how it's better, how I could use that as leverage?

"Why Jace?" I ask. Why did they want me to gain employment with Jace Barone? They couldn't have known that I'd have access to his home and his personal computer.

"That's none of your concern," Luka says with disgust. "Answer your messages." He turns and walks away into the crowd of pedestrians, disappearing in front of me.

Do I tell Jace about Luka? What would I say? Would he even believe me that it isn't my fault?

I hurry inside the restaurant and order a sandwich to go. I grab a bag of potato chips and take the items back with me to the office. After running into Luka, all I want to do is return to my desk, where it's safe. At least I think it's safe.

There are guards inside the building. It's why he didn't show his face to me at work. But how did he get the package delivered? Who at the company is working for the Caruso family? It has to be an inside job.

15

JACE

After work, I head home. Olivia is already fiddling around in the kitchen. She's chopping up vegetables, and there is a small fruit salad in a nearby bowl.

Together, we make dinner. I prepare most of the ingredients, but she helps whenever I ask her to grab something from the fridge or hand me a utensil once I point out where it's located.

Olivia's cell phone buzzes in her pocket during dinner. She doesn't so much as reach for it or glance at the screen to determine who is trying to get hold of her.

"Do you need to get that?" I ask.

"Seems rude to do that during dinner," she says.

She has a point. Is she trying to teach me manners that I'll hand down to my kid? I do tend to look at my phone a lot. It's part of the business, not just running Barone Industries but also the mafia.

It requires a lot of my time.

How the hell I'll raise a kid and find the time to change diapers, feed the little one, I'm not sure. I'll probably have to bring on a nanny full-time. Which will be fine. Olivia's room will be vacated by then, and the nanny can move in.

I smile, silence my phone, and shove it into my pocket. While I wasn't checking it during dinner, it was on the dining room table.

Her face burns. "I'm sorry! I wasn't saying that you can't look at your phone." She is quick to apologize.

"No, you're right. It's rude to be on your phone during dinner or when someone else has your undivided attention." However, I am curious who is reaching out to her.

I'm sure she has friends, family, someone who is checking up on her. But she hasn't told me about anyone else. As far as I know, she's an orphan, which I doubt is a fact, but it seems that way.

She scrunches her nose and laughs. There's a lightness to her demeanor, yet I can also see a struggle cross her features that I can't explain. I don't know her well enough to read her like a book. At least not yet.

With time, I'm confident I'll know everything about the woman carrying my child.

"Now that it's official," I say, gesturing toward her, the fact that she's pregnant, "I started ordering practically one of everything for the baby. When you start seeing dozens of packages delivered to the house, you'll know why."

She laughs and covers her mouth with her hand. "You don't even know if it's a boy or girl yet!"

"Doesn't matter," I say. "I can donate anything I decide not to keep to a charity for single mothers. I'm sure there's one out there somewhere."

She takes another bite of her dinner, smiling and shaking her head. She doesn't appear the least bit upset by my remark, which is good. "Always thinking ahead," she muses. "You should probably buy a crib at the store and not online."

"Why?" I'm curious about her thoughts. She's a mother, and while she might not have custody of her child, she probably knows more about kids than I do.

"You can't tell how sturdy or durable the crib is online or in a catalog. We went overboard on the nursery when I was pregnant, although I'm sure you'll put my buying habits to shame."

I frown. Could the caller have been her ex-husband? Does she ever get the opportunity to speak with her son? I'm sure it's a touchy subject, but Olivia never speaks about either one of them.

"Do you speak to your son often?" I ask.

Is that who had been calling her during dinner? If it was, I can't imagine she'd have ignored the caller. She doesn't seem like the kind of mom who would ever ignore a phone call or text, no matter the hour or how busy she might be.

Her face falls, and she drops the fork, the metal rattling against the table. Olivia's eyes widen, and she grabs the utensil, her cheeks red. "I, uh, he's dead, Jace."

My stomach flops.

I had no idea.

"I'm so sorry." There's nothing I can say to console her, to take away that pain. I don't ask her any further questions.

If she wants to tell me about him, I'll listen. But I don't want to push her away.

She nods, her eyes downcast on the remainder of her uneaten meal. Olivia picks at her food with her fork. Her appetite seems to have vanished.

Mine has too.

"I'm sorry," I repeat. I hadn't intended to upset her or make her the least bit uncomfortable.

"Yeah, I think I'm just going to take a hot bath and get ready for bed."

"Sure, I've got the dishes," I offer. The last thing I want is for her to be stressed during the pregnancy. That doesn't help anyone, and I don't want her emotional state to cause her to miscarry, if that's even a possibility.

She takes her plate to the kitchen and cleans it in the sink before disappearing down the hallway.

With a heavy sigh, I grab my phone. There are a half dozen missed calls and texts from Matteo.

I wait until her bedroom is closed. While I can't see her room from the dining room, I hear the clasp of a door being shut.

Standing, I grab my dishes and clean up the rest, dumping them into the sink. I skim through the texts. There's nothing specific from Matteo, just *call me back* or *urgent*, and my favorite, *pick up the damn phone, boss!*

I dial Matteo, skipping the voicemail. He doesn't leave me messages of any value. Just to call him back. I know his routine.

"Finally!" He sounds exasperated.

"What's going on?" I ask. "Why the urgency?" If he's calling me repeatedly within an hour, something is wrong. I try to hide the worry in my voice and remain calm. Maybe he's overreacting.

When has Matteo overreacted?

Other than bringing Olivia on as a surrogate, that was quite unconventional. I give him slack on that one time.

"We've got a problem. There's been an incident down at the docks."

I clear my throat and glance down the hallway, making sure I'm alone. There's no sign of Olivia. "What kind of incident?" I ask.

"The Carusos caught one of our capos."

"Shit." I curse and wince. "Who?" I ask. I trust my men, but I can't help but worry. Secrets need to be kept, and torture can be a persuasive method to gain information.

Will he divulge information at the hands of Caruso and his thugs?

"Andrea," Matteo says.

"How did this happen?" I need every detail. Mistakes like this can never happen again. Not on my watch as don.

"From what I've gathered, Andrea was followed down to the docks. One of Caruso's men tailed him during a shipment pickup."

I pinch the bridge of my nose and exhale a heavy sigh. Andrea knows more than he should. He's a vital part of our organization. I can't afford to lose an asset, but what's worse is that Don Caruso is holding him.

"What do you suggest we do?" While I don't take orders from Matteo, I do appreciate his insight. Sometimes he offers a unique perspective, and I want to hear his recommendation before I rattle off my orders.

"As much as I like the guy, he won't talk."

"Are you sure?" I value Matteo's input, but I can't help but worry that anyone can be manipulated to divulge secrets. Especially those who have intelligence information that could hurt our operation.

"Reasonably so, sir."

"If we leave him in Don Caruso's hands, he's as good as dead," I say.

I hate losing men, especially good men. But going to war over one man being nabbed would be far more dangerous and riskier. It could destroy everything that I've achieved.

And that's Caruso's power move.

He wants to destroy me and bring my empire crashing to the ground.

"Mounting a rescue mission could put more of your men at risk, dozens more," Matteo says.

I agree, but doing nothing shows weakness. It proves to Luka Caruso that he can do whatever he wants. That he runs this city, and that's furthest from the truth.

"And sitting idly by while he slaughters my men isn't something I'm willing to accept," I say. There's a firmness to my tone, a brashness to what has happened is still itching through me to retaliate.

I don't like knowing that my men, my family, is in danger.

I offer them protection, and if I can't do that, I'm as good as dead.

"I understand, sir. You asked for my position. The safe move is to let things settle and counterstrike when they are least expecting it," Matteo says.

He's a sensible man, but he doesn't understand what is at risk by waiting and not responding. Caruso will act again, and he needs to be stopped.

At all costs.

I hear the door clasp shut.

"Olivia?" I call out. I'm a bit on edge after the news Matteo just dropped into my lap.

Olivia doesn't respond.

"I'm going to have to call you back, Matteo."

"Sure thing, boss."

I end the call and shove the phone into my pocket. The lights are on in the hallway, and the alarm is set. It hasn't gone off. I'm sure that I'm overreacting, but Caruso is not to be trusted.

If he can get to one of my capos, a man trained to kill, then he can get to Olivia.

I hope I'm being paranoid.

This place is a fortress. He shouldn't be inside these four walls, but I can't help but worry.

I stalk down the hallway. Olivia's bedroom door is open. There's a private bathroom connected to her room, so I'm surprised the door isn't shut. Unless she's seeking my company?

Doubtful.

I'm overreaching.

We're just friends. Colleagues. I'm her boss. That's it. And she's carrying my child, but it's not romantic. Not that I don't have feelings for her, but I haven't acted on them. I'm not a complete asshole.

I poke my head into her bedroom.

The bedside lamp is on. It emits a soft amber glow across the room, shadows dancing over the walls and bed. But there's no sign of Olivia.

The bathroom door is also open.

My stomach tenses.

"Olivia?"

Okay, now I'm concerned.

Where the hell did she go? She couldn't have just up and disappeared. The windows are shut. The front door is locked. Hell, she'd have had to walk past me to head out the front door.

Unless she snuck out the back door. But why? And the alarm would have sounded. The keypad didn't indicate anyone turned on or off the alarm.

The door to my office creaks open, and Olivia steps out, staring at me wide-eyed. Her hand is bunched into a fist.

Is she hiding something? Did she steal something from my office?

"What the hell are you doing?"

16

OLIVIA

Jace closes the distance between us.

Shit. Shit. Shit.

I did not expect to sneak across the hall and get caught.

What do I tell him?

What excuse can I use to get my ass out of hot water?

He asked me a question, demanding to know what I was doing, and I've yet to answer.

There is no good answer that he's going to like to hear. I feel like a deer in the middle of the highway with oncoming traffic.

I'm frozen, and he's about to plow into me.

I'm so dead.

"Think carefully what you intend to say," Jace warns.

He's pissed. It's not just his tone indicating that he's mad as hell. It's the vein bulging in his neck, and his face is bright red.

"I'm sorry," I stammer.

"For?" He's waiting for an explanation, but there isn't one that I want to give. At least not one that is honest. He'll hate me, fire me, and I don't even know what would happen regarding his child that I'm carrying and our arrangement.

I need that money.

It's my way out of this debt to Caruso.

My only way out.

"I shouldn't have gone snooping." It's not a lie, but is it enough?

He flinches, and his gaze tightens. "Did you find what you were looking for?"

My mouth is dry. I shuffle my feet, uncomfortable under his scrutiny. I'm not sure what I was looking for, only that Caruso wanted me to copy files onto a flash drive, which is tucked into my palm.

I'm trying to be casual about my hands tucked into fists.

"The documents in your office, you own shell corporations?" I shouldn't be asking, but I'm curious now that I've looked. It's like opening Pandora's box. I can't put the damn lid back on quick enough.

"I own many organizations and several corporations," Jace says. "What is your question?"

"Are they all legal companies?"

He scoffs at my question. "If they weren't, don't you think the FBI would come knocking on my door? I'm in the public spotlight, Ms. Summers," Jace says, referring to me by my last name. It's cold, impersonal. That's probably the point. He's distancing himself from me.

Is it because I hurt him? Betrayed his trust? Or another reason?

He strides closer, stepping well within my personal space. Jace grabs my wrist and brings my hand up to his face, prying open my digits.

He steals the flash drive from my grip. "I'll be taking this," he says.

I open my mouth, but I don't know what to say. I'm sorry would probably be a decent start, but the apology doesn't surface. I'm both embarrassed and ashamed of my behavior, but my actions aren't who I am or what I stand for. I've only acted in such a manner because I have no other choice.

Caruso isn't a kind or generous man.

I have to hope that Jace can and will forgive me.

"Care to give me any explanation at all?" Jace's eyes are wide as he pins me with his gaze. He's waiting for me to say something.

Shock.

It's the only rational thought that explains why I've lost my voice. My heart is pounding wildly. Fear pulsates through me, mixed with a heavy rush of adrenaline.

Is he going to kick me out, force me to be homeless like I'd been before I met him?

I wouldn't blame him. He deserves to kick me out. Maybe I should suggest that I leave. Wouldn't that be better? Then, Caruso can't keep hounding me for information. I can't give him what I don't have access to.

"You'll be angry with me," I rasp. It takes every ounce of strength to speak the truth.

His gaze is intense, stern. It makes me uncomfortable.

I drop my focus down to the floor. It's easier not to meet his harsh stare. He grabs my chin and juts it up, forcing me to meet his eyes.

"Explain!" His words are sharp.

A shiver courses through me.

"Luka Caruso," I whisper the words.

Does he know of the mobster?

Jace is a billionaire. He doesn't dirty his hands in mafia politics.

"What about him?" Jace sneers.

Is it possible that he's heard of him? It's not as though the Carusos are a quiet group of mobsters. They rough up neighborhood businesses, force them to pay a protection tax or send their soldiers out to rob the storefronts.

It's no secret they're a gangster of trouble.

I exhale a shaky breath, and Jace releases his grip on my chin and my arm, letting me go. He waits for my explanation.

I contemplate running, but how far would I get? I owe him the truth. Maybe he can find a way to protect me if he doesn't hate me first and hand me over to the authorities for stealing from him.

"I'm waiting." Jace isn't the most patient man, especially when it comes to betrayal. He is well within my personal space, and I refrain from taking a step back.

"My ex-husband, John, he borrowed tens of thousands of dollars from the mafia. He took out a loan and never paid it back in full. When John ran off, Luka Caruso kept harassing me for the money. He offered me a payment plan with an exorbitant amount of interest, but if I paid every week, he'd let me live. Six months later, John returned and made my life even harder. I was managing the payments. I was making ends meet for Austin and myself. But John wanted to come back home. I should never have let him return. He was watching Austin the night of the fire," I say.

I take in a sharp breath. I won't elaborate. The memories are still too fresh, too raw.

It's easier to disassociate. Maybe it's not healthy, but it's how I deal with what happened. It's the only way that I know how.

"John died in the fire. Austin didn't succumb to his injuries immediately. Instead, he racked up hundreds of thousands of dollars in medical bills from his burn injuries before he passed. The medical bills kept piling up. The hospital didn't care that my son and my husband were dead. The mafia didn't care that I had medical expenses and I couldn't pay the mortgage. The bank took my house, and the debt collectors took every penny that I earned. There was nothing left for the mafia."

His tongue darts out and licks the corner of his lips. Jace seems lost in thought. Does he believe me? It's the truth, everything I've said. I've never lied to him.

"Luka Caruso is a dangerous man."

I'm aware of that fact, and it's why I'm terrified of him. "I know! Do you think I want to be indebted to him?" The man practically owns me. At least he thinks he does. And I can't just walk away from him. He won't let me. I've tried.

"Did he ask for you to go snooping into my office?" Jace asks. He takes a step back and folds his arms across his chest. His stance, while closed off, is more relaxed than earlier. It's a strange mixture, like he's trying to decide something, but I'm not sure what.

"He gave me the flash drive and demanded I copy files from your personal computer."

There's no point in lying to him. I've already been caught. All I can hope for is his forgiveness, and maybe he can help me out of this mess.

17

JACE

I want to punch something.

Someone.

Mainly that asshole Don Caruso. He deserves a beat down. But I can't just walk up to his compound and knock on the front door.

It's more complicated than that, but if he's been watching Olivia, maybe it doesn't have to be.

"How has he been contacting you?" I ask. I need to know everything about their relationship. I wince, praying it is in no way intimate.

Olivia did sign a contract to abstain from relations with any other men while trying to get pregnant with my child.

Her head is bent down, her gaze on her feet.

"He called my phone, had a package delivered to the office, and threatened me earlier today on my way to lunch."

I bunch my hands into fists at my side. Why couldn't she have accompanied me to lunch when I invited her? At least that scumbag wouldn't have approached her if I had been with her.

"You need a bodyguard."

It's the first order of business tomorrow morning. One of my men will accompany her anywhere she goes that I'm not with her. Whether it's doctor appointments or out to lunch, I won't let Caruso get to her again.

"Is that necessary?" Olivia asks.

"Absolutely!" Her protection and safety are of the utmost importance. Doesn't she realize that, if not for her sake, then for the baby that she's carrying? "You're pregnant with my child. That makes you a target."

She glances up at me with her bright blue eyes and expels a soft puff of air. "Okay." She doesn't fight me.

I'm not sure why I expect she would, maybe because she doesn't seem like the type of girl to give in. She's always been opinionated, at least since I've gotten the opportunity to know her.

"Tell me about this package that he had delivered to the office." I reach for her elbow and guide her to walk with me to the living room to have a seat. This conversation isn't about to wind down, and I'm not letting her sneak off to bed without answering.

I deserve that much, considering her betrayal.

Anyone else, and they'd have been killed.

She doesn't put up a fight in the slightest. Olivia accompanies me to the living room and sinks into the plush sofa.

I sit beside her, leaving ample space between us. I glance at the kitchen. I could use a drink, something stiff to help settle my insides down. Adrenaline pounds through me, causing my heart to slam against my ribcage. It takes everything inside of me to sit as if I were calm.

I'm not feeling the least bit calm or settled, but I don't indicate to Olivia otherwise. I have to be cool and collected. It's part of being don, not letting my men or my enemies see fear or uncertainty.

"There wasn't much. A note threatening that I need to answer my phone, which I left at your house on purpose. He's been texting me, bothering me, nonstop," Olivia says.

She appears genuine, and her demeanor doesn't show me that she's hiding anything. I've seen squirrelly men glancing away, avoiding my stare. Her shoulders are slumped, a sign of defeat, not defiance.

"Anything else?" I ask.

"The flash drive," she says and points at the device in my palm. "I don't know what he expected me to do with it, and I didn't plan on doing anything. But then he threatened you."

"Me?" I laugh at the absurdity of the threat. Wasn't she doing this to protect her ass? That had been my expectation. I wouldn't fault her for saving herself. It's not as though she knows how to deal with men like Luka.

Olivia slowly glances up to meet my stare. "Yes, he thought we were sleeping together since I live here."

I breathe a sigh of relief. At least he didn't manage to hack my lawyer and discover the paper trail between Olivia and me or find any records with my information from the surrogate agency who I had previously contacted.

"I see," I say. He should believe we're an item. Then he won't be surprised by a visit when I show up and threaten his ass for bothering my girlfriend. "I'll deal with Caruso. He won't bother you again."

Besides, I still need to deal with the capo, Andrea, who has been taken. It's one crisis after another.

Her voice is timid, fearful. "How?"

Is she worried that something will happen to me? She doesn't know I run the mafia, that the Carusos are a rival family, and this gives me an excuse to slaughter their men. They took one of my own. They threatened the woman carrying my child. It's time for retaliation.

Anything less, and I'll appear weak.

18

OLIVIA

He hasn't spoken about Caruso since the night he caught me in his office with the flash drive. All he said to me was that it was done, and I was safe.

What was done?

Did he kill Luka?

The man was a monster, but murdering another man doesn't make it right.

It's probably the hormones and pregnancy brain giving me crazy fantasies of what Jace did to force Caruso to leave me alone. I want to believe that he's gone and can never bother me again, but I still have nightmares about him threatening me.

Jace is a billionaire. He probably just paid the thug off. That's what rich people do, right? Money solves all their problems.

Since the incident, I've had a bodyguard at Jace's insistence. Does Jace think that Caruso's men will come after me? Why else have someone shadow me everywhere that I go?

Will I always be watching over my shoulder for Luka?

Jace drives me to work. When I refuse, he insists that Matteo swings by on his way to the office, which is in the opposite direction.

I don't need Matteo hating me. I like my job, and a small part of me hopes that I'll be able to keep it after the pregnancy.

Matteo accompanies me to lunch if Jace isn't around or is busy. If it's after hours, there aren't too many places that I go on my own. Sometimes I go shopping, but Matteo accompanied me once, and after that, it was always another guard.

Did I bore him to death?

Good.

"I'm heading out. Are you done?" Jace asks, stopping by my desk. His days have become more typical, less late nights since insisting on driving me home.

He hovers over my desk, and I'm sure the rumors are starting to spread. I've barely started showing, but any day I'm going to pop. My work slacks are already challenging to get on, and while I'd like to blame it on my eating habits lately, it's probably the fact I'm very much pregnant.

"I don't know, am I done, boss?" I ask with a smirk.

We may not be dating, but it does feel like there's something between us, aside from the little bump.

"Come on, and I'll walk you out," he says.

I shut down my computer and grab my coat, sliding it on as I hurry around my desk.

He presses the elevator down button as I approach. "How about we grab a bite to eat and do a little shopping?" Jace asks.

I don't have the slightest clue what he wants to buy. Am I tagging along because I don't have another ride home or because he genuinely wants to spend time with me?

"Shopping?" I'm thrilled with leaving now, and it's nearly five o'clock anyhow.

"Yeah, stuff for the jellybean," Jace says as the elevator doors open. He gestures for me to step in first before he accompanies me, the doors shutting behind us.

The elevator is empty. I'm grateful for the privacy between us. Well, aside from the security surveillance, but I don't think they can hear us.

Can they?

"Pretty soon, jellybean is going to be the size of a watermelon," I chuckle.

"Yeah, not before it's a lemonhead first."

I'm pretty sure the baby is already bigger than a lemonhead. Maybe it's the size of a lemon. I'd have to pull out the baby book to see how big the little one already is, but I've been trying to avoid the emotional intimacy and connection.

I want to be happy for Jace when I hand over his son or daughter, not sad. I'm sure it's a mixed bag of emotions, and with the hormones the way they are, it will inevitably be a rollercoaster.

"What's with you and candy?" I tease. I've never seen him snacking on candy. Sure, he's had some junk food in his house, but he mostly eats healthy, and everything he cooks is always nutritious.

"I like my sweets." The elevator descends to the parking garage, and Jace escorts me to his car, opening the door for me.

He really doesn't have to do that, but I smile and rather appreciate his charm. It's chivalrous.

And while I shouldn't find anything he does sweet or attractive, it's hard not to notice him when I see him every night.

I buckle my seatbelt, and he jogs around to the driver's side and climbs into the vehicle.

"Where are we heading?" I ask again. His shopping comment is way too cryptic for Jace. It's the kind of answer I'd give to one of his bodyguards when they're forced to accompany me.

"Dinner, and I'd like your opinion on a few baby things." He pulls the car out of the parking garage.

Traffic is heavy, but his attention is on the road while we converse. His hands are on the steering wheel, careful as he pulls out into traffic. He's a calm driver, far calmer than I am while in city traffic and dealing with idiots.

"Oh," I say, surprised he wants my involvement. I rest a hand on my belly. I haven't felt the baby kick yet, only slight flutters barely noticeable, but having been pregnant before, I pick up on the more subtle movements.

"Is that okay?" He's already heading away from the house, but I'm not the least bit nervous. I trust Jace.

What I don't trust is my ability not to flirt with him.

Jace is handsome, incredibly wealthy, and the most generous man I've ever met. It's hard not to fall for someone constantly lavishing you with attention. That's probably how my slight crush started.

At least, I like to think that it's small, like the size of a lemonhead. It was probably the size of a jellybean last week.

Shit.

The kid is growing as fast as my crush.

Jace glances at me, awaiting an answer. He looks concerned that I haven't told him that I'm okay with going out to look at baby things with him.

"Yeah, sure," I say and smile, genuinely excited to be a part of this process. "I just didn't think you'd want my opinion."

"You're a mom. You've been through this before," Jace reminds me. "This is my first time."

I smile weakly. I am still a mom. Even with Austin gone, that doesn't change anything. "You'll be a great father," I say, and I mean it.

He's been wonderful to me, generous. I can only imagine him being great with his son or daughter.

"Thanks, but you have to say that. I'm paying you," Jace teases.

He is paying my salary with the company and an additional stipend per month for the pregnancy expenses. Of course, it's a little more than just expenses. The extra zeroes on the checks are far more generous than any agency would provide for the surrogate.

"Even so, it's true." I smile and glance out the window. Is it warm in here? My cheeks feel heated. I reach for the thermostat. "Do you mind?"

"Make yourself comfortable," Jace says.

―――――

After a fancy dinner where I feel underdressed, even in my work attire, Jace drives us a couple of blocks to the nearest baby boutique.

It's expensive, high-end, and honestly, no one needs to spend thousands of dollars on a rattle or silver baby shoes that the newborn can't wear.

There's over the top, and then there's looking to blow money because they see you coming and know you're a billionaire. I don't let him buy anything and drag him out of the store in under five minutes flat.

"I thought we were shopping?" Jace's brow is tight. He doesn't seem to grasp what a baby needs and what a store wants to sell you.

I laugh under my breath. "You can't be serious!"

"What? You didn't think the little jellybean needs a gold pacifier?"

My eyelids narrow, and he grins.

"How about I take you somewhere," I say and hold out my hands for the car keys as we walk back to his vehicle.

"You want to drive my car?" he asks. "You could just give me directions."

"You could just hand me the keys," I say.

Why is he being stubborn? It's just a car, and he has plenty more in his garage.

Jace jingles the keys just above my hand for a second before I snatch them into my palm.

"Come on, I'll take you shopping, but I don't know what you need or where you intend to put it at home." The man has already spent the equivalent of my salary on baby purchases online.

He chuckles under his breath. "Point taken, but I still want to get out tonight."

"Oh, so this was your way to get me out on a date?" I tease as I approach his car. I unlock the doors and let myself into the driver's side.

His eyes widen, and his ears redden at my suggestion. "I wasn't suggesting this is a date, Olivia. If I wanted it to be a date, I'd have been forward and asked you out."

A smile falls from my face as I climb into the car and get behind the wheel. "Right," I say.

I avoid his stare as I adjust the mirrors and then start the engine, pulling out into traffic.

The car practically drives itself. I hadn't realized that when I'd been the passenger. "I've taken a pause in dating," Jace says.

I'm not sure why he's explaining his dating life or lack thereof to me; maybe because I put him on the spot.

"It's fine. It's not any of my business," I say. I head toward the nearest big box store for baby things. While Jace has practically everything in terms of setting up the nursery, there aren't many clothes that he's purchased. A few outfits for a newborn, but an infant can go through multiple changes of clothes in one day.

"While it may not be your business, I feel like I should explain," Jace says.

I let him talk while I focus on the road and getting us to the destination.

"You're living under my roof, carrying my child. It wouldn't feel right bringing random women home."

"They don't have to be random," I say, shooting him a look. Is that all he does, sleep around and have one-night stands?

19

JACE

There's an obvious tension between us, and I'm not sure if it's because Olivia thinks that I sleep around or if I missed the mark entirely.

Was it a bad idea to invite her to go baby shopping with me?

I like spending time with her. That shouldn't be a crime. She's fun to be around in a way that I've never experienced before.

I don't usually keep women around. It's not that I despise dating, but it's hard when everyone knows you're wealthy. Women typically throw themselves at my feet for my fortune.

They don't want me. They want what I can offer them.

Olivia is different.

It's what I like about her. From the first time we met at my office, she didn't look at me like I had the key to the kingdom and an entire treasure she could get ahold of. Sure, she knows I've got boatloads of money, but she's oblivious to the other powers that I hold.

Especially, the darker ones that are far more sinister. It's best to keep her in the dark.

What she doesn't know won't hurt her. Isn't that the truth?

"You're quiet," Olivia says as we stroll alongside one another under the harsh glare of fluorescent lighting.

I'm pushing a cart, not because I'm planning on buying anything specific, but because it seems the right thing to do. I don't expect Olivia to push the cart.

I purse my lips. "Do you have enough maternity clothes?" I ask.

She cocks an eyebrow and stops walking. "We're not shopping for me," Olivia says.

She's right, but I don't want to admit it. I keep strolling down the aisle for the newborn clothes. It's too early to tell whether it's a boy or a girl.

Do I even want to know the sex before the baby is born?

I want a son, an heir to the Barone family, but raising a kid. Fuck. I don't know a damn thing about how to do that.

Why did I think being a single father was a grand idea while also being a don?

What the fuck was I thinking?

Olivia snaps her fingers in front of my eyes. "Where'd you go, Jace?"

She can't know my doubts and fears.

Don Caruso is still out there. I have a security detail on Olivia anywhere she goes. I have my men shadowing me everywhere I go.

Except they don't live with me. They didn't need to.

My house is separate from my work.

The compound where my men live, interrogate ruthless savages, and command the city isn't far from my home. But I like to keep business separate from pleasure. And my house makes it easy to bring women home for a wild night without a thousand and one questions.

At least it did until I met Olivia.

She doesn't know about the compound, and I don't intend on her discovering it, either. There's no need with the protection that I've put on her, a bodyguard everywhere that she goes. It's a necessity after learning about Luka's threats.

I'd kill the bastard if I could get inside his home without being detected. But it isn't that easy. He has dozens of men, ready with guns to slaughter me.

Wordlessly, I wander with the shopping cart toward the newborn apparel. "Any hints on whether it's a boy or a girl in there?" I offer her a smile. It's friendly and warm, but all I feel is fear.

I do my best to mask the doubt, the fear that follows me as a mafia don. She never has to know the truth.

I keep telling myself that, willing it to be true.

She rests a hand on her abdomen. "Hard to tell," she says and scrunches her nose with a grin.

Behind her, several feet away, are two of Caruso's men. They're watching us from a distance and waiting to make a move.

She's oblivious to their presence, and I don't want to worry her. But we can't just stand here and wait for them to close in on us. They're not stupid enough to make a move inside and physically hurt Olivia or me. But they could force us outside, and that's where danger lurks.

Caruso's men have no idea who Olivia is to me. They think she's another woman whom I've bedded, but certainly, discovering us in the baby aisle will get word back to Luka.

I pull her against me, rough and forceful. It's an act, a show for the men watching. Our bodies are pressed tight, my hand's on her lower back. I long to cradle her ass, but I refrain from enjoying this. As much as I want to, there's too much at stake.

"Jace?"

It's no wonder that she looks taken aback. I've never shown any interest in her romantically, but I have no choice but to make the men watching believe that she's mine. Indeed, they will return to their compound and report that the girl is, in fact, my girlfriend.

I have to make it convincing.

And while I don't want to put her in danger, I've already done that by cruising the baby aisles. I may as well show them she's mine. Discovering she's a surrogate could be far worse, because the only thing standing between us is that baby.

I'm a bastard for putting Olivia's life on the line instead of my child.

I pull her tighter, harder, and my lips crush hers. Claiming her and letting everyone see that she's with me, under my protection.

I vow to protect the woman carrying my child, but above all else, I vow to protect my unborn child. The baby she's having—my heir to the Barone throne.

20

OLIVIA

He kissed me. Jace Barone actually kissed me.

And damn, did it feel good—my stomach flutters with butterflies. My heart soars as though I'm floating high above the clouds, and just as quickly as it starts, the heat and passion, it's done.

Jace pulls back and wraps an arm around my shoulders. "Let's get out of here," he says as he steers me away from the shopping cart, abandoning it as he directs me toward the exit.

"Okay," I whisper.

My lips tingle from the kiss.

Jace is a really good kisser. Like he knows how to make my insides stir, and my body falls under his spell.

I don't dare ask why he kissed me. I don't want to break the trance.

Am I dreaming?

I don't care if it is a dream. It's wonderful. A dream come true. Maybe he's realized that his feelings for me aren't just about having a baby, but something more.

Jace escorts me to the car, opens the front door for me, and waits until I'm buckled before he shuts the door and comes around to the driver's side.

He's an absolute gentleman.

Is it because he's going to be a father?

Does he want me in his life?

The minute Jace slams the door shut and starts the car, he revs the engine, and we tear out of the parking lot. Smoke and dust kick up behind us.

He's in a hurry.

"Sorry about that kiss back there. I had to make it convincing."

"Convincing," I say, repeating his words slowly. The fog is settling, but I don't have a clue what he's yammering on about.

"I can't let anything happen to that little one you're carrying, and there are dangerous men always watching me. They're always going to be watching you. That's why I hired a bodyguard to accompany you everywhere, but it's not enough. Not by a long shot. Not with news that you're pregnant. We just have to make sure it's convincing that we're in love and this isn't a business arrangement."

My head feels like it's spinning.

"Jace, what the hell are you talking about?" My stomach tenses. My hands quiver, and I shove them against my lap, hoping that he doesn't notice the slight tremor.

Everything I ate for dinner tumbles in my stomach.

Please, don't let it come up.

"Caruso's men were watching us back at the store."

"What?" I gasp. The car is warm—sweat beads on my brow. I roll down the window, needing air.

Jace hits the button to shut the window and then locks all of them from the button on his door. "It's not safe."

I want to get out of the vehicle.

Run.

Flee.

Is this because of Luka Caruso and the debt that I owe him?

No, that doesn't seem right. It doesn't feel right. Luka is a man after money. He's threatened me in the past, and I'm sure he's capable of intimidating me, but whatever is going on inside of Jace's head doesn't feel the same.

There's a slight quiver in my voice. But I demand to know the truth. "How is it not safe?" I ask.

I need answers.

He owes me the respect of telling me the truth.

"Caruso wasn't aware of your pregnancy. You're not showing," he says, glancing at me. "Not yet."

He returns his attention to the road, his knuckles tight as he grips the steering wheel. Every so often, he glances in the rearview mirror.

Are we being followed?

It's dark. I don't see any headlights in the side mirror, but I suspect Jace is better at ditching someone tailing him. Though I don't know why he'd have any experience doing that, he's a billionaire, not constantly being chased by bad guys.

"I don't understand. You said you'd take care of things with Luka Caruso."

I hadn't asked what he'd meant by that, but I had assumed he'd gone to him with a boatload of money, threatened him, and insisted that Luka leave me alone.

Was that not what happened?

"It's more complicated than you think," Jace says.

"You don't know what I think. Tell me, Jace, what the hell is going on?"

We weave through back roads and side streets until we eventually end up in the heart of downtown. There's a tall wrought-iron gate. It's seemingly familiar, like whoever designed this place designed Jace's home.

There's similar architecture to the building behind the guarded fence. But it's bigger. Much bigger. It makes Jace's home look like a cottage compared to the mansion stretching across acres of land.

Jace pulls up to the entrance, and a guard clicks a button, unlocking the gate.

"Where are we?" I ask. Again, my voice quivers.

There's a lot I don't know about Jace, and I shouldn't care. It shouldn't matter. We're not dating. Hell, we're not even a couple.

I'm his business partner, the surrogate for his child.

But I feel a darkness that I can't explain looming over this place—like a fortress, guarded and protected.

But why?

"Who are you?" I whisper, glancing at him. My mouth is dry—my stomach tenses. To say I'm nervous, would be an understatement. I'm terrified.

Jace is keeping secrets. But I don't know why. He owns a huge corporation, and he's a billionaire. It would make sense that he'd have elaborate security measures and guards. This feels more like the home I expected to see when we first met. Not the little cottage across town.

But it's darker, heavily guarded, and something feels off.

Is it a decoy house?

Is that even a thing? I exhale a loud, heavy sigh.

Jace parks the vehicle and steps out. He comes around to my door and opens it. I haven't so much as moved an inch. I'm still buckled into the seat.

"Come on. We need to get you inside."

My gaze travels over the exterior of the building. It's old, but beautiful. The exterior is brick and well-kept. There are three stories, and the building towers above us.

"I'm not going anywhere until you tell me where we are," I demand.

He owes me the truth.

He sighs and reaches into the car, leaning over me as he unbuckles my seatbelt. "I have a second house. You can either walk inside or I'll throw you over my shoulder and carry your ass into the house."

His gaze latches on mine.

"I'll walk," I whisper, staring up into his sharp green gaze.

"Good."

He pulls back long enough for me to climb out of the vehicle. He slams the door shut behind me before I have time to close the door. Jace's hand is on my lower back as he firmly escorts me up the stone stairs.

"Is this your fortress of solitude?" I joke. He doesn't strike me as a superhero. There's something dark about him, about this place.

"Something like that," he whispers as he escorts me to the front door. There are biometric readers on the outside of the building. A retinal scanner, handprint, and voice imprint. "Jace Barone." His words are a command, and the door unlocks for him.

All that security, and he couldn't just have a guard open the door? It seems a bit like overkill, but what do I know?

"Evening, boss," Matteo says with a nod as he greets Jace.

Boss?

I've seen Matteo at the office. I didn't realize the job extended outside of business hours. The poor guy, forced to work all day and night.

"Let me take Olivia upstairs and show her to her new accommodations. I'll be back down to discuss matters," Jace says.

Matteo gives a firm nod.

"Accommodations?" I ask. I thought I was staying with Jace?

Is this where his business associates stay? Is it a retreat center?

I don't recognize anyone else from the office, although Jace employs quite a lot of people. There are many men, all in business suits, a few with earpieces in. They look like guards. They all have a gun holstered to their hip.

"Yes, this is where you'll be staying," Jace says as he leads me up the stairwell.

The mansion is huge. The floors are hardwood with a narrow staircase that curves up to the second level.

I follow behind Jace, taking in my surroundings. There are paintings on the walls, masterpieces. Originals. They must be real, considering Jace's fortune.

He leads me down the hallway, which appears to stretch on forever. I'm sure it's an illusion. To the right, he opens the door and gestures me into the room.

"I'll have your clothes brought from the house," Jace says.

Stepping into the bedroom, I can see that it's massive. The room is larger than my apartment, which seems insane for a bedroom. There's a balcony outside that stretches across the length of the bedroom and a view into the courtyard.

"Is that a garden down there?" I ask, gazing out the window. It's stunning. The courtyard is large enough to house a swing set when the little one gets older and is protected from danger.

Was that Jace's plan? To keep his son or daughter always safe?

I suppose I'll be staying here until the baby is born.

"It is," Jace says as he comes to stand beside me. He opens the window, allowing fresh air to resonate through the room. "What do you think?"

It's not bad, but I refuse to admit that I'm impressed. "I thought I would be living with you," I say. That was the agreement, and while I wasn't interested in playing house, this place scares me. Probably because of the dozens of armed guards I've seen already. Doesn't this place put me in further danger?

"You will. I'll be living under the same roof. As we grow closer to your due date, I'll also be bringing in a midwife in case you need any additional care or go into labor early."

I don't know what to say. He's not breaking the contract, but why show me his humble abode and make me live here with him? He still hasn't answered me about Luka Caruso. He promised to take care of it.

"Why are we moving here, now?" I ask. "Did Luka Caruso threaten you too?" It's the only logical explanation that I can make sense of. Why else would he worry about those men at the store tonight?

They were following us. Jace had seen it. He probably has been trained to take notice of suspicious people and situations. Being a billionaire must come with a lot of threats. I can only surmise that Luka is after his fortune.

But Jace is an honest man, making an honest living.

"He's always a threat."

My gaze tightens as I turn with my back to the window and fold my arms across my chest. "There's something you're not telling me." I can feel it, the heaviness and uncertainty looming over me. Whether it's intuition or just plain common sense, he's hiding something from me.

"You're right, but it's for your safety," Jace says. "I can't protect you all the time. This way, you and my child are always safe."

My mouth is dry, parched. "And that kiss earlier. What was that?" I ask.

I need the truth.

Was it all an act?

Am I a fool for believing he feels something for me?

21

JACE

I was hoping that she wouldn't bring up that kiss we shared. Not because it wasn't amazing and passionate. It was probably one of the most intense kisses that I've had, but it wasn't real.

She's not mine.

It was all an act. And apparently, we're both good at pretending.

Except she wasn't pretending. She didn't know I was acting on impulse to save her. Protect her. Well, to protect my unborn child.

The kiss ignited a spark inside me, and now with every glance at her, my insides stir, my body reacts to her.

It has to be the pregnancy. She may be hormonal, but she's also carrying my son or daughter.

It's the only explanation.

I mean, sure, she's beautiful, sexy as hell, and has a great ass. But it's more than that. There's a familiarity between us, like we're old friends. It's comfortable. Easy. I don't have to pretend to be someone else around her.

Not that I've divulged the real me, either, but from the pieces that I let her witness, we merge seamlessly.

"Jace, are we going to talk about that kiss or just pretend it never happened?"

Part of me wants to pretend it didn't happen because that would be easier. But I have to face the fact that I kissed her, and even if it was just an act to protect her, I enjoyed it.

"I kissed you because I don't want rumors starting with the Carusos."

Her brow tightens, and the corners of her lips frown. She pouts.

It's rather cute.

"What kinds of rumors?" she asks.

"Luka's men have been watching you, following us. They assume we're together, and I don't want it getting out that I hired and paid for a surrogate."

"I don't understand why it matters, but I respect your decision to keep it private," Olivia says.

"Thank you," I say and turn for the door. I need to have a word with Matteo, ensure the compound is secure, and have one of my men return with Olivia's belongings from my house.

———

I shut her bedroom door and step out into the hallway. Matteo is waiting for me.

I accompany him down the stairwell and to the war room. It's where all our meetings of importance are held. There's equipment to ensure nothing is overheard and no signals go in or out of that room.

"I wasn't expecting you to bring the girl by the compound," Matteo says.

I shut the door behind him once we've been allocated our privacy in the war room. We're not at war today, but we might as well be. Every day, it seems as though there is a new battle. Some, we win, and others, we live to fight another day.

"We were being followed. I couldn't chance taking her back to the house. Besides, Caruso's men saw us shopping for baby things." I wince at my own words. I'd been careless. I should have brought multiple guards with me. Usually, I have more than just one or two bodyguards following me, keeping eyes on me so I don't have to watch my back.

But I'd been swept up in the moment, enjoying spending time with Olivia, and had allowed her to take me shopping.

It had been my idea. I don't blame her. I blame myself.

Matteo grimaces. "Does she know who you are, that you're don?"

Does he expect that she'll find out while living under my roof at the compound? I don't plan on her discovering the truth. In a few months, she'll be gone, out of my hair, and I'll never have to see her again.

There's a sadness that grips my gut when I think of the future and her not in it with me.

"Of course not." I laugh under my breath. It's absurd for Matteo to think I'd tell Olivia the truth. He knows I'm good at keeping secrets. Unless they're my family, I don't trust easily. And while I don't think Olivia would betray me, I don't know who she might confide in.

I've had a lifetime of learning to keep secrets, of hiding who I am, and that I run the mafia.

"And she won't find out," I reiterate to Matteo. I don't expect him to divulge our little secret.

"What about work? When she starts showing, is she going to be able to keep it a secret that the kid is yours?" Matteo asks.

He's always had doubts. Of her loyalty, whether she was up for the job. Hell, he didn't think that I should hire her.

I'm glad I didn't listen to him because I might not be having a kid in a few months if I did.

"I've got it handled." He needs to worry less about my personal life and more about Luka Caruso and to make sure that rat stays far from the compound and far from Olivia.

22

TWENTY WEEKS PREGNANT

OLIVIA

It seems like I barely see Jace. He's busy with work or getting the new house prepared for the baby. He's had everything from the other home brought over for the nursery.

Sure, we share a meal at night, and he drives me to and from work when he's in town, but spending time with him outside of business is few and far between these days.

Will he live in the mansion after the baby is born, instead of his other home?

Why have two properties so close together? Usually, a person's second home is like a vacation home, some place far away. Both properties are within driving distance.

It's obvious the man has a treasure trove of secrets, but they're not mine to delve into. I respect that I can't and won't know everything about him. But I know enough.

He's genuinely a good person. Jace would go to the ends of the Earth to protect his child. And that's good enough for me.

I practically waddle as I walk. The baby is growing faster than I would have thought, and I swear I look nine months pregnant, but I'm nowhere near ready to deliver. Maybe I just feel incredibly self-conscious about the fact I'm carrying someone else's child.

The girls at the office have asked when I'm due, who the father is, the whole shebang. I avoid as many questions as I can, and I've never divulged that it's Jace's or that I'm a surrogate. Maybe I should tell them the last part, because won't they want to see baby pictures?

That assumes that I come back from maternity leave to work at the reception desk. Which I don't think I will.

It'll be better, a clean break. Besides, Jace is paying me enough that I can invest in myself, maybe do something I like for a living instead of making ends meet.

There's an art gallery where I'd love to apply to be a curator. Even more, my dream would be to paint and sell my artwork, but I haven't done much painting lately.

And there would be no questions if I start over—a fresh slate.

Jace stops by my desk, a cup of coffee in his hands.

I breathe in deeply. I can smell the savory aroma from the coffee. I haven't touched caffeine in weeks. I'm doing everything that I can to ensure the healthiest baby that I can for Jace. I rest a hand on my abdomen, feeling a slight flutter.

"Is he doing somersaults?" Jace asks, a wry grin as he brings the mug to his lips. Like he's trying to hide the smile on his face. His eyes still shine just as brightly.

"Yes, on my bladder," I say with a chuckle. "I'm about ready to head out." We have a doctor's appointment, and Jace insisted on accompanying me, which is fine since it is an appointment regarding the little nugget growing inside me.

I shut down the computer and stand. I step around my desk and join Jace near the elevator. He's careful to keep his hands to himself, but to me, it's so obvious that something is going on between us.

Whenever I go anywhere, either Jace or Matteo accompanies me out of the office. I'm sure the rumors are spreading like wildfire, but no one has said anything to my face.

Besides, in a few months, I'll be gone. This will all be behind me.

The elevator dings, and Jace holds it open, letting me step in first.

I wait until the doors shut and we're alone before speaking my mind. I don't need to offer up any rumors, either. "Do you want to know the sex?" I ask.

We haven't talked about whether we should find out at the doctor's appointment, but the last time we went, they said we should think about it, we didn't have to decide anything right away.

"Do you?" he asks.

I laugh under my breath and roll my eyes. It's his kid. It doesn't matter what I want. I'm doing this for him. "Nope, that decision is entirely yours," I say, resting a hand on my belly. "You're the father."

His tongue darts out along the edge of his lips, like he's thinking something but not speaking. He's not one to hold his tongue, which just makes me further frustrated.

My hormones have been terrorizing me, desiring him day and night. It's madness, and that simple little gesture is driving me crazy. "Well, make up your mind," I snap.

I expect him to take a step back, to avoid me at all costs. But he doesn't.

His eyes crinkle with mirth. "Okay."

Okay?

That's all he has to say for himself? Inwardly, I groan. But it's not as quiet and in my head as I thought.

Jace raises an inquisitive eyebrow. "Something wrong?"

"Yes. No." I can't tell him the problem is that I've had sex dreams practically every night. I was tossing and turning, waking up, aching for the touch of a man.

And not just any man.

It's always Jace.

"Just haven't been sleeping very well," I say. He's waiting for an answer.

And I hate myself for it. As much as I don't want him to know, a small part of me, in secret, wants him to find out. Then, maybe he'll indulge my fantasies.

But I know that's all they are and can't ever be anything more.

He's a billionaire. I'm just a girl having his kid. It's a business transaction. That's it. Plain and simple.

Except, it doesn't feel that way, living under his roof. It feels like more, and I know it's all in my head, but I can't help the way he makes me feel.

Undeniably, I'm crazy in love with my boss.

Okay, it's probably the hormones talking. Still, it doesn't negate the fact I dream of Jace naked daily, his body teasing mine, always hovering, never satisfying me completely.

It's torture.

And maybe that's why I'm frustrated with him. It's the dream version of Jace who has worked me up and hasn't gotten me off. It's not the real Jace's fault. I know, I'm crazy. Insane.

Again, blame the hormones.

We walk to the parking garage in silence. His hand rests on my lower back as he escorts me to his vehicle and opens the door for me.

Always a gentleman.

I grumble under my breath.

"Is the bed not comfortable?" Jace asks. "I can have a new mattress ordered and brought into your room."

He slams the door shut, comes around to the driver's side, and starts the engine. Jace glances at me, waiting for an answer.

He really is clueless. It's sweet. Rather endearing.

My bottom lip curls between my teeth. I'm trying everything I can to refrain from speaking the truth, from telling him something that can't be unheard. Because once it's out in the open, that's it. It can't be undone. And my humiliation will be everlasting and long.

"The mattress is plenty comfortable. I promise it's not anything with your home."

"Then it's me?" he asks.

He doesn't avoid the hard questions, does he?

I exhale a heavy sigh. "Can we just not talk about it?" I glance out the window—anything to capture my attention and focus the conversation on anything else. And I mean anything. Zombies. Childbirth. Maybe not the two of those things together.

Right now, I'd settle for a zombie apocalypse to save myself from discussing my desires with Jace Barone.

But I'm not so lucky.

"I just want to help," Jace says. His voice is soft and soothing, calm. Like he's really worried about my well-being. He's probably concerned about the pregnancy.

He reaches for my hand and gives it a soft squeeze. The gesture is my undoing.

"You can't help. The hormones are intolerable," I say. I glance at him, praying he understands what I'm saying without having to elaborate. Could this be any more humiliating?

"Oh," he says slowly, like it's starting to connect. "You're horny?"

My cheeks must be red because the car feels a hundred degrees hotter. I'd roll down the window, but the last time I did that, months ago, he got snippy. Instead, I reach for the thermostat and adjust the temperature.

"I wouldn't put it quite like that," I say. He makes it sound crude. It's not like I'm prowling the town for a man. Hell, I haven't even bought a vibrator to satisfy my desires. Maybe I should. That would at least help me sleep. But I worry the men inside the house, the guards, might hear me.

There's a silence that follows. I'm not sure if he doesn't know what to say or has decided it's best to refrain from speaking any further. After all, he is my boss.

———

"Olivia, how are you doing?" Doctor Morgan asks.

I'm situated on the uncomfortable beige bed in the exam room, with the crunchy paper tucked between me and the fake leather.

"Fine," I say.

Jace stands beside me, eager for the ultrasound.

"I'm sure you must be excited to see the baby. Do you two want to know the sex?" Doctor Morgan asks. She's barely looking at my chart. Instead, her attention is on preparing the equipment. She squirts a nice glob of jelly goo on my belly.

At first, it's cold, but the discomfort is quickly gone. Well, most of the discomfort. I had to drink a ton of water before the appointment, and my bladder is about to burst.

Is this a cruel pregnancy test? See how long a pregnant woman can hold her bladder before exploding?

"Yes, we'd like to know the sex," Jace says.

The doctor moves the ultrasound wand across my abdomen, bringing the little nugget into view on the screen. "How have you been feeling?" Doctor Morgan asks.

"She's had trouble sleeping," Jace says, answering for me.

I eye him strangely. He doesn't need to speak for me.

"That's not uncommon. If anything, later in your pregnancy, you'll find it's harder to get comfortable. How about your hormones? Have you noticed any changes in your desire for sex?"

I want to die.

Is it possible for the doctor to stop talking? I don't answer, and Jace takes it upon himself to respond for me.

"She has seemed moody lately," Jace says. "She mentioned being horny."

"Those were your words! Not mine." I can't believe the nerve of him. I could kill him!

The doctor smiles warmly as she continues with the ultrasound, oblivious to my humiliation. Or maybe she's used to couples bickering during appointments. "It's completely normal and quite common to have an increased sex drive during pregnancy. It's healthy and natural to have sex while pregnant, and there are plenty of positions that you can experiment with to make sure the mother is comfortable."

I swear I'm dying of embarrassment, and Jace doesn't say a word.

He smiles and nods, like he's listening, practically taking notes. Is he enjoying this brand of humiliation directed at me? He doesn't appear the least bit embarrassed or uncomfortable.

How is that possible?

I'm going to kill him later!

The steady rhythm of a heartbeat pulses through the internal speaker.

"She has a strong heartbeat," the doctor says.

"She?" Jace whispers as his eyes light up.

"Yes, that's right. It appears you're having a baby girl. Congratulations."

A huge grin spreads across Jace's face. I want to wipe the smile from his lips for humiliating me with the physician, but he's happy, and I don't want to take that moment away, either.

"A girl," I whisper, smiling weakly. I'm truly happy for him.

And by the looks of it, he's excited too.

———

"Can you believe it's a girl?" Jace asks as he escorts me back to the car.

"Well, it was fifty-fifty," I say with a smirk.

Sitting beside Jace, there's a calmness that envelopes the car. Silence.

It's getting late, and rather than return to work, he's heading us back toward his mansion in the city. I've gotten used to the new house. It's roomier, not that I need a ton of space. The garden is lovely when the weather cooperates, and there's always someone around. I never feel lonely, even when Jace is working late.

Although most of the guards aren't overly friendly, Markus is always at my side, accompanying me on walks whenever I travel away from the mansion.

While Markus is quiet, he doesn't ignore me. If I speak to him, he answers. Unlike Matteo and Vincent, who spend more time staring into oblivion, making sure we're not being followed.

Are that many people after billionaires?

Did Jace steal their blueprints or something to create his company? I swear there's a bigger secret, but I can't quite figure it out, and snooping around the office or the mansion is not an option.

I've already been caught once, and I wasn't sure Jace would ever trust me again. And I can't just come out and ask him. He wouldn't tell me about a secret like that unless I liquor him up. Tempting but unrealistic. I rarely see him drink.

"Can we stop on the way home for ice cream?" I ask. Suggesting a bar is out of the question. But I want to get out, celebrate the good news.

"Won't that spoil your dinner?" Jace asks.

Already he sounds like a parent.

"No, I'm eating for two," I say. In case he's forgotten. I doubt he has. My belly is already growing, and I've been moody lately. "Satisfy a pregnant woman's cravings."

Jace raises an eyebrow.

Shit.

I didn't mean sex. Well, sure, I'd be agreeable with him scratching that itch, but I don't expect him to follow through with it.

"Which cravings are we talking about?" Jace asks with a smirk.

He loves torturing me.

23

JACE

I hate to admit that I like flirty Olivia.

There's something primal about her carrying my child, looking sultry and seductive. Even when she's not trying to be sexy, she's irresistible.

Olivia doesn't answer me when I ask her which cravings she wants me to satisfy. I've tried to tread carefully. The last thing I want is for her to throw a sexual harassment suit at me.

She wants me to stop for ice cream, but it's already growing closer to dinner. I'm a bit hungry for dinner, and I imagine she is too. "Ice cream is after dinner," I remind her. "I can have Markus or Vincent make a run after we eat, to bring you whatever flavor of ice cream that you crave."

Olivia grumbles under her breath.

She doesn't sound the least bit satisfied or pleased with my suggestion. I thought after the long day with work and at the doctor that she'd want to put her feet up, relax.

"We can watch a movie together after dinner," I suggest. I want her to unwind, and if she isn't sleeping, whatever the cause may be, she isn't taking care of herself.

"Promise me it won't be a guy movie."

"What's a guy movie?"

"Blood, guts, gore. Action with no plot."

"I'd like to think the movies I choose have a plot," I say. But she isn't wrong about my typical selection. "We can watch whatever you want, even if it's a chick flick."

She scrunches her nose most endearingly. "And you'll have melted ice cream delivered?"

I pull up to the house, and the guard at the driveway entrance unlocks the gate. I give him a brief nod and a wave of thanks. "It won't melt. It's freezing outside," I counter.

"Well, the car will be warm."

It's like she's trying to pick a fault with everything I suggest. I exhale a heavy sigh. Bringing her here was my idea. Having her live under my roof. "If you want me to take you out after dinner for ice cream, I will."

"Thank you." Her smile brightens up the car.

I swear it's like dealing with a child. Is this what I get to look forward to when my daughter is born? Of course, she won't be eating ice cream straight away, but the constant neediness and attention.

I groan.

This is exactly what I signed up for, isn't it?

————

After dinner, Olivia and I head to the car. With the sun setting, she grabs a heavier coat, but the buttons don't secure. It's getting too small with her round, pregnant belly.

"Are you sure I can't convince you to stay in, and we can order dessert?" I don't mind going out into the cold. But she isn't appropriately dressed for the weather.

"No chance of that. Your guards will bring back grocery store ice cream. I want the good stuff where they smash in brownies and mix it up in front of you."

Well, at least she's not craving pickles in her ice cream. Smashed brownie does sound pretty good.

I grab an extra beanie from the closet and pull it over her head, ensuring that she is warm and toasty.

She whips out a set of gloves from her pocket and slides them onto her hands. At least those still fit.

We head out into the cold. The car is already heated and running, thanks to Markus starting the engine.

In a matter of minutes, I park the car and step out to help Olivia out of the vehicle. "No bodyguards?" she asks. "How come I always require a bodyguard, but you never do?"

It's not true that I never have a bodyguard with me, but I'm also highly skilled and trained to handle situations. There are times I have men accompany me places, especially when arrangements have been made in advance and someone might be aware of my schedule. But on impromptu visits like to the ice cream shop, it's unlikely we'll be followed.

"I'm not the one with Luka Caruso threatening me," I say.

That's not entirely true, but it should be enough of an answer to keep her from asking any further questions.

"I thought you said he wouldn't bother me anymore," she quips. She isn't wrong, that is what I assured her, but it wasn't because I offed the man. If it were that simple, I'd have put a bullet in his head a decade ago.

"He won't bother you because you have a bodyguard everywhere that you go," I say with a sly grin. I open the door to the ice cream shop and escort her into the building.

It's comfortable inside the shop, the heat is blasting, and I remove my gloves and hat while Olivia does the same.

She hurries up to the counter and gives her order. I follow behind her, picking out my concoction, and pay the attendant. We grab a seat at the table near the back. The place is relatively empty, not that I'm surprised because of the weather. I'm more shocked that they're open.

Taking a bite of her ice cream, she scrunches her nose. The gesture is quite adorable.

"Brain freeze?"

"You would think," she says with a laugh and shakes her head. "The baby is kicking. Do you want to feel?"

Before I have time to answer, she grabs my hand and places it on her belly.

"Can you feel that?" she asks.

I'm not sure what I'm supposed to feel. Her coat is unbuttoned, but she still has a lot of layers on.

Olivia must sense my frustration as she moves my hand and presses it harder, covering my hand with hers. I feel a slight flutter against my palm. It's slight, barely noticeable.

I almost wonder if I imagine it, except she's laughing and grinning.

"Wow."

"I know, right? It'll be more noticeable when she starts somersaulting and doing gymnastics, which is what my son did in the last trimester. The kid barely let me sleep."

"Worse than now?" I ask.

Olivia pins me with her stare. "It's not the baby keeping me up at night."

———

After dessert, we head back to the compound. We remove our jackets, hats, gloves, and shoes. It's probably overkill. I've lived in colder climates, but I don't want to chance Olivia catching a cold while pregnant.

I accompany Olivia up to her room. It's her private sanctuary with a television, bed, easel, and even a mini refrigerator was brought in so that she wouldn't have to roam around the compound.

That was my doing. It's best if she doesn't see what's going on right in front of her.

And I want her to be happy. She told me she likes to paint, so I made sure to buy her an easel and deliver supplies weekly to her room.

With winter on the cusp, there's little reason for her to venture into the garden, which means her bedroom is where she spends most of her time.

While we were out grabbing dessert, I texted Vincent to have a massage table brought up to her room but to ensure it was equipped for a pregnant woman.

Olivia needs to relax, and maybe I can help her calm down.

"What's going on?" she asks as I follow her upstairs. Usually, I give her space and privacy in the compound.

"I have a surprise for you," I say.

"Did you finish setting up the nursery?" Olivia asks. She's trying to guess what I might surprise her with, although I'm not sure why the nursery would be a surprise for her.

I don't give any indication of what I've got planned. "A few weeks ago. Guess again," I say.

"Movie night?"

It's a good guess, considering we had discussed watching a movie to unwind for the night. "That's not the surprise, but we can have a movie night after the surprise if you're still awake."

"I give up." She opens the door to her bedroom. A massage table is situated in the center of the room, across from her bed. "What do we have here?" She glances at me over her shoulder. "Did you hire me a private masseuse?"

Will she be disappointed when she finds out that I planned to give her a personal massage? Maybe I should have hired someone so that it wouldn't be deemed inappropriate.

Fuck me.

She's staring at me with that seductive sparkle in her gorgeous blue eyes, waiting for me to answer.

"I was going to give you that private massage. Unless you're uncomfortable and I could ask one of my men—"

"No!" she blurts before I can finish my sentence. I'm not sure whether she thought I was going to suggest one of the other men watch or give her a massage. It doesn't make much difference.

I try not to chuckle at her outburst. "How about you head into the bathroom and get undressed? There's a robe hanging on the back of the door for you to change into."

"You thought of everything," Olivia says as she saunters into the bathroom.

I remove my blazer and loosen my tie. It's still warm in her bedroom. I undo a few buttons on my dress shirt. I want to wear something far more casual, but I'm too lazy to head across the hall. I'm also concerned if I do leave the room, Olivia might change her mind.

I'm thrilled with the prospect of giving her a massage and touching her. I shouldn't be this excited, but she's carrying my unborn child. Something is thrilling and scandalous with the fact she's my employee, and everything we're doing has been kept a secret.

How much longer can we keep this secret from the world? The media will be hounding my office soon enough.

The door clicks, and Olivia slowly saunters out, the white terry-cloth robe pulled around herself. She's holding it to keep me from getting an eyeful. It's big and was supposed to be a maternity fit, but I didn't exactly know which size to get for her.

"Where do you want me?" she asks. There's a smirk on her face, like she's trying to flirt with me but cautious at the same time. She could easily excuse her comment as innocent if need be.

"On the bed—the massage bed," I clarify and clear my throat.

What is wrong with me?

Oh right, my member is growing hard just looking at her in a robe. How pathetic is that? Not that Olivia isn't sexy because she is, but she isn't even showing an inch of skin.

I shouldn't be this reactive to her near-nakedness. Of course, it doesn't help that I've been celibate for months since she moved in with me. A guy has needs, and mine aren't being met.

Long, cold showers don't do it justice.

I want her.

But I won't cross that line without her consent, and even with it, I don't want to ruin what we have. It's perfect. She's carrying my daughter.

If I fuck this up, I don't know how she'll react or what she'll do.

She's pregnant, and while I recognize that she's not fragile, she is hormonal. I don't want to be the cause of a very pissed-off Olivia Summers.

"Do you have a sheet or something that I can cover up with?" Olivia asks.

Her innocence is sweet and rather endearing.

It takes everything within me not to pounce on her.

"Yes," I say and retrieve a white cotton sheet that was folded on the side table with the massage oils.

"Would you turn around?" She gestures with her finger for me to turn and face the opposite direction.

I turn to face the door, giving Olivia her privacy while she disrobes. There's a soft thud of the fabric hitting the floor and the rustle of the sheet as she covers herself. "How am I supposed to lie on this table?" she asks.

"On your side," I suggest. "I have some special pillows that we can use to make sure you're comfortable." I wait to turn around. "Do you want me to grab them for you?"

I hear the soft creak of the massage bed and the jostling of sheets as Olivia climbs onto the massage table.

"Okay, I'm well, decent. I mean, I'm naked, but you can turn around."

She sounds nervous.

I can't hide the wide grin on my face, even if I wanted. "You look pretty decent to me." She's lying on the table on her side, the sheet covering her body.

I reach for a pillow, offering it to her to make herself more comfortable.

"Thanks," she says. "Do you have another pillow for my head?"

"Planning on taking a nap?" I tease. I grab a pillow from the bed and bring it to her, helping her get comfortable. "Better?"

"Much."

I step around the massage table so that I'm behind her. "Sorry if my hands are cold," I warn before grazing her skin with the lightest of touches.

My fingers caress her shoulders, and she slinks down into the pillow, holding it against her chest as she shimmies the sheet down her back, letting me get a more intimate glance at her back and the curve just before her perfect ass.

This should be off-limits, giving a full body massage to your employee.

Her skin is porcelain and creamy, speckled with a dusting of freckles that matches her nose.

I squeeze a generous amount of massage oil into my hands and rub them together before letting my hands work on her shoulders and back.

The soft, subtle sigh of content falls from her lips.

"Is that okay? Is it too much pressure?" I ask, wanting her to enjoy the massage and not feel like I'm hurting her.

There's a slight moan as she shifts subtly on the massage table. I presume she's trying to get comfortable.

"No, you're fine. It's good," she says as she hugs the pillow to her chest, hiding her breasts from my view.

What I wouldn't give to be that pillow nestled up against her body, hugging her curves.

This is supposed to be about her, though, not my needs. I may need to get laid, but Olivia needs sleep. And me sporting a hard-on while massaging her isn't going to do either one of us any good.

Thankfully, she's facing the opposite direction.

"I hope this is helping you relax," I say as I massage her shoulders and down her back.

Her body seems to relax beneath my touch, and the tension that I initially felt dissipates. Whether it was nerves from me giving her a massage or it's helping her unwind, I can't tell the difference.

Olivia mumbles something unintelligible into the pillow as she clutches it against her chest.

"What's that?"

"I feel like I've died and gone to Heaven. Your hands are amazing," she says.

I want to show her how amazing I can make her feel, but she has to tell me I'm what she wants. I won't cross that line without her explicit permission.

My touch is feather-light and gentle, grazing up her neck as I sweep her hair up and pin it to her head with one hand. The other hand teases along her jaw. "So, I've been told," I joke. I want to kiss her, but I don't. It's not out of fear. There's little I fear. It's a matter of respect.

She rolls onto her back, clutching the pillow, keeping herself hidden from me. Her long lashes flutter as she stares up at me. Her cheeks are rosy, her blue eyes dark. "Don't laugh."

"About?" Why would I laugh?

"I can't take the hormones any longer. If you don't sleep with me, I need a vibrator, or I want one of your men to come into my bed. I swear I'm about to touch myself in front of you just to see if you'll give me the real relief that I need with this massage."

I promised I wouldn't laugh. But the smile on my face is huge. Wide. "I want to kiss you. I've wanted to kiss you from the first time we met," I confess. I lean closer, my lips not quite grazing Olivia's yet. "But I didn't want to force you to do anything with me, ever."

It was never about not wanting her. It was about respect, giving her the power to make that decision.

Olivia leans into the kiss, and my fingers rake through her hair, pulling her closer, her lips tighter and harder.

Her lip's part, and her tongue eagerly searches my mouth, fueled with want and need. She's fire, and I'm the coals to stoke her flames.

"You are not sleeping with any of my men," I say. And I mean every word. She's off-limits to them. If any one of them comes near her to satisfy her sexual cravings, I'll kill him.

"Does that mean I get to sleep with you?" Olivia asks with a sly grin.

My fingers delve beneath the simple cotton sheet, and her legs instantly part for me. My hand is warm and firm, sliding up her thigh, teasing her. "Only if that's what you want," I say.

I can just as easily satisfy her without the two of us fucking.

She pulls her bottom lip between her teeth. Is she nervous?

We shouldn't be doing this, at least not on the massage table.

The woman carrying my daughter deserves a good experience, with being ravished and adored. Not fucked awkwardly on the massage table just to get her off.

My fingers graze her sweet lips before pulling away.

Olivia whimpers in protest.

"Oh, we're not done yet, sweetheart. I just want to make sure you're fully enjoying the experience." I help her off the table.

"Where are we—" Her words are cut off when I guide her to the mattress and bend her forward over the bed. "Oh," she gasps. The blanket falls around her feet on the floor.

She's breathtakingly beautiful with her swollen belly and breasts. I come up behind her, one hand caressing her breast, the other sinking back down between her thighs.

Olivia gasps and breathes deep, leaning forward on the mattress with her arms, giving me the perfect view of her ass. I want to unbuckle my slacks and fuck her, but that's not what I'm going to do.

No.

I want her first experience while pregnant to be entirely about her, for her enjoyment.

"Tell me what you like," I whisper against her neck. I drop soft butterfly kisses over her skin. "You've had sex dreams. Tell me about them."

Her breathing comes out raspy and in pants as she tries to speak. I'm pressed up against her, one hand gently squeezing and caressing her breast, teasing her nipple as her hips rock back into mine.

My other hand strokes her wetness, teasing her pearl as she begins to shudder in my arms. I've barely touched her. I haven't even used the entire length of my fingers, and she's trembling and moaning as she speaks.

"They're always you," she says.

I squeeze my digits together, putting mounting pressure on her clit as she moans and gasps, her hips bucking against me. I slide two fingers into her tightness and curl my digits with each thrust.

"Oh God," Olivia pants, one hand clenching the bed sheets, the other reaching around trying to touch me.

I bend forward, covering her, touching her, feeling her body against mine. "Come for me," I whisper into her ear, sucking the lobe as I continue my ministrations on her body.

Her insides clench and spasm, the first wave of an orgasm coming to the surface.

I don't let up, wanting her to ride out the orgasm as little ripples flutter through her body.

She gasps and pants, trying to catch her breath. "That was—" she rasps, glancing at me over her shoulder.

"Incredible," I answer for her.

24

THIRTY-FOUR WEEKS PREGNANT

OLIVIA

It's been four days since I've seen Jace. He's been away on business, insisting on traveling overseas now to finalize all the details of his merger before the baby is born.

Why he has to wait until I'm thirty-four weeks pregnant is beyond me.

Jace swears he moved the deal up and that it'll be a short trip to Italy.

What I wouldn't give to travel to Europe. Well, not in my current condition, with swollen ankles, a huge pregnant belly, and my bladder constantly being crushed by the little gymnast inside.

I've taken maternity leave a little early. While the doctors haven't insisted on bedrest, they did recommend that I take it easy. And at Jace's instance, I packed up my desk, which leaves me a lot of free time at the house.

I stalk down the stairs. The weather is blustery outside, but I want to get a little sunlight and fresh air.

"Where are you going?" Matteo asks.

He didn't accompany Jace on the trip to Italy, but he does talk to him every day, constantly reporting on my condition. Jace could just call me, but he doesn't.

"Outside, for a walk." I zip up my parka, which is huge and fluffy. It's plenty warm and will be a waste of a decent coat when I'm no longer pregnant.

"It's freezing outside, and you're pregnant."

I scoff. "It's Los Angeles, not Antarctica. Besides, the doctor said that fresh air and taking a walk are good for me. You can't keep me locked up in this place just because I'm pregnant."

Matteo grumbles under his breath. "Markus!" he shouts to the younger guard.

Markus hurries toward us from down the hall. "Yes, sir?"

"Escort Olivia on her afternoon walk. Be back before sundown," Matteo says as he glances at his fancy watch.

Matteo dashes around the corner and into a nearby office, leaving me alone with Markus. That's fine with me. He's much easier to deal with if I have to bring a guard with me.

"Help me with my shoes?" Reaching my feet is problematic with my round, pregnant belly in the way.

Markus doesn't object. He's quick to offer me a seat on the bench near the door. Within a few short minutes, he's got my shoes on, secure, and then helps me to my feet.

"Thank you," I say. I grab the beanie from my jacket pocket and slip it on before sliding my hands into my gloves.

Markus wears little more than a black coat and boots. There's no hat or gloves. Is he trying to show he doesn't need those things?

"Where are we heading?" Markus asks as he escorts me outside. "Your usual route?"

There aren't that many ways to tour the neighborhood. Once past the gates, the road goes east and west. After a half-mile, there's another street that connects and offers a different path.

I'm not sure how much walking I have in me with the little one pressing on my bladder, but I want to see sunlight before it's dark. I hate how dark it gets earlier in the day. I loathe winter.

However, after being contained in the mansion and without many places to go, the outside keeps looking better and better.

The guards open the wrought-iron gates, and we step on through. Markus glances at my feet. "You're going to need winter boots. I can't believe Jace hasn't insisted on buying you a pair. Those shoes aren't the least bit warm."

"You haven't tried them," I say. "They're lined with fur and comfortable." They are short for snow and resemble clogs that aren't particularly helpful when it's wet outside.

Markus grimaces. "Shit."

"What's wrong?" I ask as we head just past the mansion.

"I left my phone in the house. I need to go back and grab it before we go any farther," Markus says.

"You go back. I'm not going to get that far ahead," I say and rest a hand on my belly. It takes me a lot longer to walk than it used to. Being pregnant is quite exhausting, not that I don't love it, but it's harder to get around than it used to be a few weeks ago.

Markus grumbles under his breath. "Boss won't like that," he says.

"Jace doesn't have to know. I'll stay on this street and waddle a few more houses down. You'll be able to catch up with me."

Markus pinches his lips together. "Fine, but don't stray off the main road."

"When do I ever?" I ask, giving him a pointed look.

He jogs back to the gate and dashes across the lawn for the main entrance.

I continue to waddle my way down the road. It's nice to have a few minutes of peace and quiet outside to myself. It feels like forever since I've been left alone, unattended.

The silence and peacefulness are cut short.

A white van pulls up beside me as I'm walking, the back door slides open, and two men jump out, forcing me at gunpoint inside.

"Get in!" one of the armed men shouts. He's dressed all in black, except for his face. I don't recognize him, and he doesn't seem to care that I see who is abducting me.

That doesn't bode well. If he doesn't care, does he plan on killing me?

Maybe he wants to hold me hostage for ransom? If they know that I'm connected to Jace Barone, that I'm carrying his daughter, then it's possible they just want a payday.

I glance back over my shoulder. The house is just out of view from the bend in the road. There's still no sign of Markus.

"Who are you?" I try to stall.

The man pistol whips me across the face. "Get in!" His roar is deafening.

I wipe the blood from my forehead and climb into the vehicle, intentionally dropping one of my leather gloves behind for Markus to find. Hopefully, the smeared blood will give them a clue that I'm in danger.

25

OLIVIA

"What do you want with me?" I ask.

The two men in the back of the van don't answer my question. They force my hands together in front of me and bind them with duct tape.

"Silence!" they command and threaten me with covering my lips.

I agree to their silence. At least for now.

I can't see where they're taking me. The road is bumpy, and the drive seems long, but I have no idea how much time has passed.

Eventually, the van comes to an abrupt halt, and I'm shuffled out the side door and into a large building with men standing guard, semi-automatic weapons in their grasp.

What is this place?

I don't ask. I know better than to cause a scene right now. Whatever I do, I must protect Jace's daughter. She's the priority.

Luka Caruso stands in the back of the hall, arms folded across his chest. "What do we have here?" His smile is sinister and sends a shiver down my spine.

"Luka," I rasp. A small part of me had wished that when Jace had taken care of the problem with Luka Caruso, he was dead.

But who was I kidding?

Jace isn't a murderer. And it seems paying the man off didn't help.

"Welcome home, Olivia." He grabs me by the arm, escorting me forcefully down the stairs.

It's dimly lit with cement steps, and as I graze the bottom landing, there are several prison cells. "What is this place?" I whisper.

"Where you'll be staying," Luka says and opens the prison cell door. It creaks as he swings it open and pushes me inside. "Hands," he commands, and I show him the duct tape around my wrists, binding them together.

He retrieves a switchblade from his pants pocket and slices through the adhesive, separating my wrists.

"If you're holding me for ransom, you should know that Jace is out of town." I don't want to be left alone in this cold, damp prison cell. However, I don't want to be saddled up with Luka Caruso, either.

I want to go home, back to the warm mansion and my comfortable bed.

There's a cot in the corner and a scrappy sheet attached. I shouldn't have let Markus return to the house without me. Does he work for Don Caruso?

Was it a coincidence that I was left alone, or did Markus have something to do with it?

"Ransom?" Luka laughs and scoffs at the suggestion. "I don't need his dirty money. I know the accommodations aren't what you're used to, but you'll be safe here."

"Safe?" What was he talking about? "Your men had me taken! I'm not the least bit safe with you," I snarl and launch at him, but he takes a step back. He's quicker than I am and slams the prison door shut.

The metal rattles and I shove my arms through, attempting to grasp onto him, but he's too quick.

"I'm not the monster, Olivia. Your precious boyfriend, the father of your child, he's with the mafia."

I take a step backward in the prison cell, shaking my head in disbelief. "No, you're lying."

I don't believe him. Jace has been good to me, good to his employees. There's no way that he's with the mafia. He's not a mobster. He'd never hurt anyone.

"I have proof," he says. "Just stay right there." Luka winks as he heads for the stairs.

Fear grips me. Uncertainty hangs in the air, looming closer, swirling around me like a dense fog. As much as I don't want to be anywhere near the man, the fact he's leaving scares me even more.

What if he doesn't come back? What if Luka leaves me here to rot in this cell?

I scream, not from the horror of the situation but from a contraction that rips through my body, bringing pain to the surface. "Not now," I scold my unborn child, crying out in agony.

She can't come right now.

As if I have a say in the matter.

Luka turns around, sensing my discomfort as I have one hand latched onto the metal bars and the other on my abdomen. I'm hunched forward, wincing from the onset of contractions.

They're intense. Not the least bit gentle or far apart.

What the hell is happening?

"You'd better not be faking," Luka says as he heads back toward the prison cell.

I'm covered in a sheen of sweat. "Does it look like I'm faking?" I snap. Anger resonates within me. This is his fault, bringing me here against my will. "If anything happens to the baby that I'm carrying, I'll kill you."

Luka's eyes crinkle with mirth. "Do you think I'm here to hurt you or your child? You're mistaken. We're here to save you."

I don't believe him. He has me locked in a prison cell.

He's unlocking the door, shouting to his men to come down at once in haste.

Feet pound against the cement, and my eyes are slammed shut, gripping the metal cage bars as another contraction rips right through me.

It feels like hell.

My water breaks.

Just in case I wasn't one hundred percent certain that I was in labor, it's obvious the baby is coming, whether I want her to or not.

"Call Doctor Morgan," Luka shouts at one of his men.

How does he know my physician? Does she work for the Caruso family too? Is she part of the mafia?

"I'll be quick," Luka says, hovering by me as he unlocks the prison cell.

I want to fight him, run, and escape, but the baby is coming. What I want doesn't matter.

"As I said, we're here to help you. Albeit not an unselfish decision, but you should know the truth. Hear it from me." He smiles, and all I want to do is wipe that smug grin from his face.

"Hear what?" I shout.

The pain comes and goes in short bursts, waves like the ocean crashing down on the shoreline, one right after another.

"Your boyfriend, the father of your child, Jace, he's a murderer. He murdered my father, and he's responsible for the fire that stole your son and husband."

Lies.

It can't be true. "How?" It's the only word I can groan between contractions. I don't want to believe him because if it's true, then everything I've been doing has been for the wrong reasons.

"He had bad information," Luka says. His eyes bore into mine. "He killed my father the same night your family died. In a fire. It turns out our addresses are reversed."

"No." I don't want to believe him.

He recants the address, and I gasp, falling forward, the pain ripping through me, searing and hot.

It doesn't matter that I'm not ready, that Jace is on another continent, and I'm six weeks early.

The baby is coming.

26

JACE

"What do you mean, she's been taken? Who the hell took her?" Sweat dribbles from my forehead, and I wipe it away with my handkerchief.

"We're not sure of that yet, boss. There weren't any witnesses," Matteo says.

My stomach roils. "No witnesses. Did they hit the compound? How many of my men were injured in the attack?"

"She was nabbed while taking a walk this afternoon."

Unacceptable!

"Why wasn't one of my men with her?" Everywhere she went, she was supposed to have a guard accompany her.

"She was out taking a walk with Markus. He stupidly returned to the compound to retrieve his phone. By the time he returned, she was gone," Matteo says. He's calm, much more rational and in control than I feel with the news.

"It has to be Caruso and his men." It's the only play that makes sense, Luka coming after my child.

"That's what we suspect as well. The cameras in front of the house caught a white van speeding by. There's no surveillance captured of her actual abduction, but we're confident that it's Caruso. You two have bad blood, and if he tells her about that night—"

"He won't," I snap at Matteo. The discussion regarding the past is done. We all make mistakes. Mine were deadly. "I want a team put together to retrieve Olivia and my daughter unharmed. You're in charge of the mission until I return. I'm heading straight to the airport."

I hang up the call and glance at my phone. There's been no contact from Luka Caruso.

What's his end game? Why kidnap Olivia other than to hurt me? Is that his plan, to make me suffer? Will he divulge my secrets?

He's crueler and far more cunning to just capture her for sport.

Does he want my position of power and control over my men? It wouldn't be hard for him to destroy me.

It's why I never allow myself to get close to anyone. Except I broke my own rule with Olivia. And now she's out there, in danger, and I'm to blame.

27

OLIVIA

I'm whisked off to the hospital with Doctor Morgan accompanying us in the dark van. The same vehicle they used to snatch me off the street.

She doesn't say anything, but she looks about as stressed as I feel, minus the pain of being in labor. It's clear to me that she's under duress.

What do they have on her?

Have they threatened her family?

I can't worry about her. My focus is on the little girl about ready to burst through the seams and arrive far earlier than I'd like.

The doctor is monitoring my contractions on the way to the hospital.

Each bump in the road is a new brand of torture and pain. I want to scream for the driver to pull over, but I don't think he will, nor does it matter. It's not like I can run and escape. If we do pull over, I'm at the mercy of the newborn I'm about to give birth to, and that doesn't involve running far. Maybe onto the grass.

"You're doing good," Doctor Morgan says as she studies her watch and times my contractions.

We're not alone in the back of the van. A man with a giant scar across his left cheek holds a gun in his hand. It's a threat. His finger isn't on the trigger, but he knows we are at his mercy.

We pull up at the hospital emergency room bay, and the man with the scar opens the back door while the driver retrieves a wheelchair near the front entrance.

In a matter of minutes, I'm shuffled through the hospital and up to labor and delivery. The men with the guns have their weapons hidden, but they're just a few feet behind us. Doctor Morgan is pushing the wheelchair, taking charge of me as her patient.

"You have to wait out here," she warns the mobsters as she ushers me back through the double doors.

"We have orders to stay at her side at all times," the scar-faced man says.

"I don't care. You wait out here, or I call security."

They huff and snort their discontent as she wheels me through the secure area. "Relax, they can't get to us back here."

I wish I could believe her, but they aren't going just to let me go and leave us alone now that I'm in labor.

The pain rips through me, another contraction. I have so many questions, concerns, worries, but none of them matter.

Jace isn't here.

Maybe that's for the best. I don't want him in the delivery room if he is mafia and responsible for Austin and John's death.

I don't want him anywhere near the baby.

And the baby is coming now. It feels like any minute, and the little one will be making its grand entrance into the world.

28

JACE

The flight is long and tedious over the Atlantic Ocean. There's been no news of her whereabouts, and I'm not good with waiting.

Matteo is lining up my men to break into Caruso's compound. There have been no sightings from the outside, and we don't have any men on the inside.

It's risky with such high amounts of security who will be protecting Luka. No doubt they're expecting our arrival and have ramped up their guards with extra weapons and firepower.

We're going into a bloodbath. I can only hope that most of my men come out alive.

They're well-trained, but so are the Caruso's. We weren't always enemies. We had been joined together under one leader many years ago, long before I became don.

I get word once they're inside the compound.

"Tell me you've got her."

I need good news. There's little I can do but wait and sit tight on the plane.

"She wasn't at the compound. One of the men said she was transported to the hospital before I shot him."

"Hospital?" Something must be wrong. Is it with her or the baby? Did Luka shoot her? It's too early for the baby to come. She's not due for six more weeks.

"She's in labor," Matteo says. "I'm sending Markus to the hospital to find out what's going on. As soon as you land, I'll have a chopper ready to transport you to the hospital."

"I want you watching over her room. Not Markus."

The kid royally fucked up, letting Olivia wander alone outside of the compound. None of this would have happened if he had followed my orders.

"Of course, boss. I'll head over there right away," Matteo says.

I hang up the call. My head spins. I'm grateful I'm not the one flying the plane. I sit in the leather passenger seat with my head in my hands.

It's not just my daughter's life that I'm worried about. Somewhere over the last few months, I've fallen for Olivia Summers.

I wasn't supposed to become intimate with her. She was just a surrogate, nothing more. But all that changed several weeks ago after finding out the sex of the baby, bringing her home, giving her that joyous massage.

"Jace, that was—"

"Incredible?" I kiss a soft path of kisses against the back of her neck.

She shifts around to face me, her eyes heavy and a wide grin spread across her face. "I think you've unleashed a beast."

"What's that?" I ask.

She reaches for my belt, pulling it loose, yanking it from my pants. "I want more," she says.

The boldness and brashness from her are what I've waited months to see and experience. Not just in terms of sex, but her taking charge, demanding what she wants.

"Good, because I'll give you whatever you want," I say, pinning her with my stare.

She exhales a soft puff of air. Her cheeks are rosy, and she shuffles back on the bed while I strip down, shucking my clothes to the floor.

Olivia is breathing hard, her eyelids heavy, her pupils dark and wide, leaning toward my lips. It's like this tiresome dance we've been doing for months is finally met with fireworks.

A perfect explosion.

I roll her onto her side, curl up behind her, and guide my leg between hers. Teasing her, touching her, listening to her moans and pleas. With her body nestled up against mine, it takes no time for me to become rock hard, throbbing for release.

She may have been having sex dreams, but I've been fantasizing about driving my cock into her, listening to her moans and screams of pleasure.

Each gasp as I touch her drives me wild with need.

"We don't have to have sex," I whisper into her ear.

I want to. My body is throbbing for release, but I've made it clear that this is about her pleasure, and I don't intend to do anything that would make her unhappy.

"Your needs are my needs," Olivia whispers. "Tell me what you want, Jace."

She's raspy and breathless. The sound of her voice is like music to the heavens, sweet and energetic, making my cock twitch.

"I want you," I confess, telling her that my body is hers to do with as she pleases. "But you're pregnant."

"So?" she glances back at me over her shoulder. "The doctor said we could experiment."

That is what Doctor Morgan instructed. "I've wanted to fuck you since the moment we met," I say. "But we can't have a one-night stand."

"You're the one who sleeps with random strangers. Not me," Olivia says. *She wiggles her butt against my cock.*

I groan at the excruciating torture of not yet fucking her. Talking about this with her is driving me insane. My throbbing cock can't take much more.

"I want to fuck you, today, tomorrow, for as long as you need." I refrain from telling her forever. Now isn't the time to get sappy or sentimental.

"That's good enough for me," Olivia whispers and reaches behind her for my member. She strokes the head. Her hand is warm and gentle, teasing me before I rest a hand on her wrist.

"If you keep doing that, I'll disappoint you."

There's a smirk in her tone. "I doubt that's possible." She bends her knees and shifts, giving me ample room to slide inside her warmth.

I guide my fingers between her folds and touch her, stroke her, tease her wetness before I drive my cock inside her. She's tight, and her insides pulsate the moment I enter her.

"Don't come yet," I command into her ear, kissing her.

My hand caresses her breast and down across her belly to her pearl, teasing her with each thrust.

Her back arches, and she tightens onto my shaft, growing close.

I trail a path of kisses across her neck and shoulder, sucking gently as she thrusts her hips against mine.

"Harder," she pants.

Her insides clench down onto my cock. They tremble against my member.

I quicken my pace. She's close, and I want her to ride the impending wave as long as she can.

"Come for me," I whisper against her ear, tugging the lobe between my teeth, sucking, and teasing her.

Olivia's body trembles and clenches down, her insides quivering and squeezing my cock, bringing us both over the edge together.

One night of pleasure turned into two. And soon, I was joining her in bed almost every night, sneaking in late when the lights were off and offering myself up to her, for her pleasure, of course.

But it wasn't just about her needs.

She met mine. Surpassed those needs and quenched desires I was unaware that I had until I met her.

And now, once the baby is born, what's next?

She goes off on her own, to live her life, and I'll never see her again. That isn't what I want.

But is that what she wants?

It's not a discussion that we've had. I've avoided the conversation because I thought we had six more weeks to figure it out.

I was wrong.

29

OLIVIA

She's beautiful. Ten fingers and ten toes. She's perfect, albeit tiny and fragile, weighing just over four pounds.

She's whisked away to the NICU. I don't want her to be alone. What if Luka and his men go after her?

As soon as I'm allowed, a nurse helps me into a wheelchair to spend time with my baby girl in the NICU.

It's dangerous, thinking of her as mine. But Jace isn't here, and there are men with guns just a few feet away behind a set of double doors that offer no protection.

The nurse doesn't pay them any attention as she strolls me right on by them to see my baby girl.

Markus and Matteo are both in the hallway. Neither says a word to me.

There's a sadness in their eyes. Is it regret? Anger? I can't read them.

There's no sign of Luka and his men, but that doesn't mean they're not nearby. Waiting for me.

I am escorted past both of Jace's men and into the NICU. Is it true, is he mafia? My stomach is heavy, weighed down by a lead ball tormenting me.

Why can't I have this one moment of happiness?

Although how can I be truly happy? It's not giving up the baby that hurts me as much as the fact she's still so fragile. She wasn't ready to come out into this world yet, and those monsters made her come early.

Not to mention what they said.

It all must be lies.

I blame Luka Caruso. He was behind my abduction, snatching me off the street. What he said about Jace being responsible for my family's death can't be true.

Whatever is going on between Luka and Jace, it doesn't involve me.

It can't.

Jace would have told me the truth. He wouldn't keep secrets from me. Would he?

"Have you thought of a name yet?" the nurse asks.

"She's not mine to name," I whisper.

The nurse gives me a peculiar look. "I'm the surrogate," I explain. "Her father should be here soon. He was out of the country—"

She wheels me up alongside the open incubator.

"I realize it may look scary, but the bed is keeping her warm," the nurse says. "The good news is that she's just over the threshold of being four pounds. Hopefully, she won't have to stay in the incubator for long. The doctors are monitoring her vitals and will speak with you soon."

"Thank you."

———

I cradle the little baby in my arms. I hadn't planned to breastfeed her, but I also didn't expect her to be born early. She's cradled against my skin, latched on when Jace enters the room.

"Is that her?" Jace asks. His cheeks are red, his eyes groggy. He appears exhausted.

Makes two of us. Possibly, three.

"I'm sorry. I wanted to be there when you delivered."

"I know," I say. I glance from Jace back down to the little girl in my arms. "I wasn't going to feed her like this, but the doctor said it would be beneficial, and it's easier for her to digest breast milk than formula." I offer a weak smile.

"She's so tiny," Jace says. His gaze moves from his daughter back up to me. "How are you doing?"

"Other than Luka's men nabbing me off the street?" I'm still bitter about the ordeal, but they brought me to the hospital.

It could have gone a lot worse.

Worry ebbs at me. Is it over with them? Will they be back to come after the little girl or me?

We're given a few moments of privacy. One of the nurses is across the room caring for another preemie, paying us little attention.

I pin Jace with my stare. "Is it true?" I ask in a hushed whisper. I need to know this little girl will be safe with him.

His brow tightens. "Is what true?"

I nod for him to lean closer.

He follows my silent instruction.

"Everything that Luka told me, that you're with the mafia, you burned down my house, and killed my family."

I don't want it to be true. I'm wordlessly begging him to tell me Luka is a liar and trying to manipulate me and turn me against Jace.

Jace glances down at my exposed chest. He's not so much gazing at me feeding the little girl in my arms, but something else.

I straighten my back as I'm seated with the little girl against my chest, latched on as she feeds. "Tell me the truth. I deserve it, Jace."

"It's not what you think."

I laugh at the absurdity of his statement. Isn't that what they always say? "That's an excuse. So, it's true?"

Jace grimaces. His eyes darken his mood changes with it. "What I've done in the past doesn't concern you."

"It does when you've murdered my husband and my son!"

30

JACE

This isn't how I wanted Olivia to find out.

I didn't intend on her discovering that I'd been responsible for the fire that night her family died.

It had been an accident—an easy mistake. One of my men had dyslexia and screwed up the numbers on the address.

A mistake that won't ever happen again.

He's dead.

I had him executed.

But it doesn't bring back the two innocent lives lost. Before I met Olivia, they were just a number, a body count that had been added to the tally of deceased individuals who had died in a war I didn't want to be a party to, but I'd inherited the position.

Men were counting on me. And if I didn't protect my men and the city, it would be overrun with drugs and weapons, murders, and men threatening innocent women, like Olivia.

Doesn't she see that and realize I'm not the bad guy? I'm just caught up in the mafia. It sounds worse than it is. I swear I'm not the devil. Not by a long shot.

She barely looks at me, and I worry most of all that she'll expose my secret and betray our vow, unwilling to give up my daughter that she is contracted to do so. If I take her to court, I'll win, but my reputation will be destroyed. Barone Industries will be put under scrutiny. There are plenty of fronts I have to launder money, but it doesn't matter.

Olivia has the power to destroy me.

I should never have involved her. The moment I realized the connection, the association between the past and the present, it was too late.

She was pregnant.

And now she's holding my daughter in her arms. I should be grateful she's feeding the baby, caring for her in a way that I can't, but she shouldn't be here. She's done.

Her commitment to me is over.

"You don't have to be here," I say, reminding her of the deal we had. Her end is complete. She gave birth to my daughter. "You shouldn't be here."

While I want her at my side, that isn't the arrangement.

"I'm not leaving," Olivia says, staring at me pointedly. The nurse returns, taking the sleeping infant from Olivia's arms as she lays her back into the incubator.

"Have you thought of a name?" the nurse asks, oblivious to the tension mounting between the two of us.

"Yes, Astrid Elisa Barone," I say. I hadn't known what I was going to call my daughter until I saw her, until this very moment.

"That's a beautiful name," the nurse says, jotting it down. She tends to little Astrid, making sure that she's okay before checking on the next infant.

"I thought Astrid could be named after Austin. They both start with A's." I'm trying to get on Olivia's good side.

Should it matter?

We will never have to see each other again. I'll deposit the remainder of the funds that she's due, and that's it, the end.

Olivia opens her mouth and quickly shuts it. Like she has something to say but thinks better of it.

"I'm not leaving her bedside, Jace. Not until she's released from the hospital."

It worries me, her attachment to Astrid, her loss of one child already, and what it might mean. I wasn't oblivious to the dangers when I went into this deal with her, but I didn't think she'd discover my past and who I am.

I didn't look too deep into discovering her past, or I might have thought twice about asking her to be the surrogate.

Will she fight me for custody?

We had an arrangement and a signed contract. But what will that matter if she blasts it to the media that I'm don, the head of the Barone family, a mobster?

———

There's a strangeness between us. A stillness. The calm before the storm.

Olivia is released from the hospital, but Astrid hasn't been given the all-clear yet. She's doing well, thriving, but still not gaining enough weight and able to regulate her body temperature.

So, we wait.

I have work to be at, but I've taken leave and let Matteo handle office politics and mafia leadership while I'm at my daughter's bedside. I've never counted on him as much as I do now.

Olivia is with me every day, every step of the way. I've insisted that she is free, but she doesn't leave Astrid's side, pumping and feeding, bonding with my daughter.

And it scares me.

I didn't agree to co-parent.

Astrid is mine.

But biologically, Olivia is her mother.

I was warned about traditional surrogacy and advised against it, that I should instead seek a gestational surrogate who had no legal rights to the child because her egg wouldn't be used.

But I did what I wanted against advisement. And now I'm stuck facing the consequences of my actions.

It doesn't help that I've slept with Olivia, formed an attachment to the woman who carried my daughter.

Do I want her to leave? No, but I'm also aware of the damage I've done, the pain she's endured at my hand.

"I'll pack up my things," Olivia says.

It's late, and staying at all hours of the night doesn't help anyone. I'd consider booking a hotel room near the hospital, but Astrid is stable. The doctors assure us she is doing as well as expected, and we just have to give it time.

I take Olivia back to the compound, but I have no real plan. I should be interviewing nannies. Eventually, I'll be expected to return to work, but the thought is furthest from my mind.

"You don't have to go anywhere," I say. My hands are on the steering wheel, tight.

We've barely said more than a few words over the past couple of days. Every conversation has been about Astrid.

Eventually, we're going to have to talk about us. Or whatever it is that exists.

"Staying doesn't seem like much of an option," Olivia says. "I'm sure you want your own space and me out of your hair."

I don't tell her that the thought of her leaving tears me up inside.

"The house is plenty big," I say, offering a reasonable excuse for her not to leave.

She exhales a heavy sigh. "I'll leave when Astrid comes home with you," Olivia says.

Silence fills the vehicle as we get near the compound.

"Is it true?" she asks.

"Is what true?" I want to steer clear of any conversation regarding Luka Caruso and her abduction. But we haven't talked. The hospital wasn't the appropriate venue for that conversation.

"You had my husband and son murdered."

When she says it aloud, it's like a sharp dagger pierces my heart. "It was an accident."

"But you were trying to murder someone?" Olivia presses further, forcing my hand. I don't want to reveal a world to her that's dark and terrifying, that would give her nightmares when she closes her eyes when going to bed.

"I don't take what I do lightly," I say. I've never killed anyone where it wasn't justified. Although the law wouldn't consider murder a just cause, we don't operate within the lines of the law. The police tend to look the other way. We also don't give them a lot to work with in terms of evidence.

We leave nothing behind.

That's why there'd been a fire that night. I had all the evidence buried and burned.

Destroyed.

No one would ever know or tie me to the crime. But here I was, practically confessing my sins to Olivia Summers.

This was a dangerous game.

She was dangerous, pulling the truth from me, something that I hadn't shared with anyone outside the family. Ever.

"Are you wearing a wire?" I abruptly pull off to the side of the road. I unbuckle my seatbelt and yank her shirt open. The buttons fly off. I've been betrayed before, and I can't help but doubt her questions and integrity.

"What the hell are you doing?" she shrieks. Olivia smacks my arms away. "Get off me!"

I do as she asks, only because there's no evidence of a wire, no surveillance as far as I'm aware.

She's clean.

I'm the one with my hands filthy.

"I'll tell you everything, but only when we're back at the compound." I need to know with absolute certainty that my words can't be used against me.

"And then?" she asks. "What happens to me?"

Does she fear for her life?

She should. Not that I'd ever harm a hair on her head, but it doesn't make me any less of a monster. Once she learns the truth, it can't be unheard. Pandora's box is open.

"Luka could potentially come after you again." While I don't think he will, because he won if his end game was divulging my secret to destroy me.

"He won't," Olivia whispers, as confident as I am that he's done what he intended. The damage is severe. Everlasting.

"Even so, I've set you up with an apartment in the city. The building will have private security, and you'll be safe."

She exhales a heavy sigh. "Safe like the last time, when I had some creep snooping on me?"

I grimace and fall back into my seat. I fasten my seatbelt and return onto the road. "That was different. It was Luka's men watching you."

We both think he's done. He's had his fun. At least I want to believe the game of chasing Olivia and hunting her down is over. He caught her. I lost.

And while I might have lost, she's still alive. And for that, I'm eternally grateful.

She's silent as I drive us back to the compound. Just as we reach the complex, she glances at me. "I was falling in love with you," she whispers, staring at me.

My heart hammers in my chest.

Yeah, me too.

But there's no sense in wasting air telling her I'm sorry or that I feel the same way. Apologies are meaningless. They're for the weak. And let's face it, nothing I say or do can fix all the shit I've caused and the damage I've done.

I fucked up.

She steps out of the vehicle, and I follow her inside. Olivia heads straight up to her room. "Can I get you anything?" I offer.

Just as she reaches the top of the landing, she spins around to face me. One hand on the banister, the other pointing at my chest. "There's nothing I could ever want from you."

"I never meant to hurt you," I say. It's probably the worst apology, but it's true. My intent wasn't to hurt her or her family.

"You know what, Jace? Luka was right."

My mouth is parched. I'm afraid to ask where she's going with her line of thinking. It's dangerous.

Lethal.

While I'd never hurt her, I can't say the same about him.

"He said I should keep the baby, that only then you'd know what it was like to lose your own flesh and blood, your only child."

He wanted Olivia to hurt me. I'd expect nothing less. I destroyed two families that day: Luka's and Olivia's.

Luka's father had been the mission, destroying one don to disrupt the empire, and the hope was that the two families might merge, again, under new leadership.

That was wishful thinking. It was foolish to believe Luka would accept his father's death without retaliation.

"In case you've forgotten, Luka is the monster."

"From where I'm standing, you look like one as well."

She spins on her heels and heads for her bedroom.

I follow close behind. There's so much that she doesn't know about our feuding families. My role in this wasn't by choice. It was out of necessity.

"The Carusos are violent psychopaths," I say, chasing after Olivia. I follow her into her bedroom and slam the door shut abruptly behind myself.

She jumps.

Did she not realize I was on her heel, following her?

"Well, you're a murderer," she says pointedly.

Even as she voices the words, she doesn't look the least bit afraid of me. Is she hiding her fear? Or does she realize that some men are worse than others?

"I only did what was in the best interest of the family and the city," I say.

I take her hand and lead her into the bathroom, slamming the door shut. I flip the fan and turn on the shower.

"I'm not showering with you, Jace." She folds her arms across her chest.

"You don't have to. Strip. I need to see that you're not wearing a wire. Then, I'll tell you everything."

She grumbles and slowly strips out of her clothes. It's not the easiest of tasks. She leaves her underwear and bra on. "Happy?"

"Nothing about this makes me happy," I say. I gesture for her to turn around so that I can inspect every inch of her.

She rolls her eyes, turns to show me she's not wearing a wire. There's nothing attached to her undergarments.

"Spill it," she demands.

There's no backing out. She deserves the truth and to hear it from me.

"Luka's men are dangerous. They threaten women, children, anyone whom they deem beneath them. You've seen firsthand how Luka treats a grieving widow," I say, reminding her of what she endured at his hands.

She doesn't object, only stares at me, seemingly convinced that I'm the monster in this story.

"He runs the black market of the city, kidnaps young children, especially newborns, and sells them to an adoption agency that he owns."

That had been my initial fear when Olivia had been taken—that Luka would sell my child on the black market.

"I don't care about his crimes. I realize he's an asshole. What I don't understand is how you lied to me for months! You climbed into my bed, pretending to be a hero when all you are is a monster."

She isn't wrong. I wish she were. If I could undo all of it, maybe I'd try something different.

"I can't let him own the city," I say, ignoring her anger and resentment. She may forever hate me. It's something I will have to learn to live with and accept. "He steals children, and he sells guns and drugs. Then he threatens small businesses, demanding they pay for protection, or his thugs loot the place."

"And you're what, some type of hero?" Her words are marked with disdain.

"I'm no saint, but I'm not Luka Caruso, either," I say. "We have a few casinos underground that aren't the least bit legal and run under the radar, but we're not hurting anyone. We offer protection from Caruso's men to the businesses that need help, and I run a network that is capable of handling fake papers and identification."

She scoffs under her breath. "You mean to tell me that's the only illegal business dealing that you do, gambling and fake IDs?"

"We have an underground BDSM club," I say with a smirk.

"I'm not sure whether you're joking or not." Her gaze tightens, and she holds up a hand to silence me from responding. "I don't want to know. I get it. Luka is a bad man. You're what—a saint?"

"No, I'm just not the devil you have me pegged to be."

She huffs under her breath. "Fair enough. I still hate that you killed my son, my husband. I can't let that go. Don't expect my forgiveness. Not now. Probably not ever."

I press my lips together. "I understand." I try not to stare at her nakedness. I want to touch her, hold her, make up for my past transgressions.

I'm not an idiot. I know sex is off the table. Not only because she just had a baby, but because she'd probably chop off my dick if I came anywhere near her with it.

She's pissed at me, and forgiveness isn't an easy thing to accept, especially from a man running the mafia.

31

FOUR WEEKS LATER

OLIVIA

I've avoided Jace as much as I can, but that's an impossible feat when he's driving me back and forth to the hospital, at my side with Astrid.

I should probably relinquish my rights as promised. And I will, but not before I know that she's safe.

She will be safe with Jace, right?

He's the head of the mafia.

How can she ever be safe? I don't even feel safe, and I'm still sleeping under his roof. I don't feel safe from him, his men, or Luka, who is still out there.

Will Luka Caruso return for me?

I haven't seen him since the day I was taken, the day that I delivered Astrid. I am constantly looking over my shoulder at the hospital. Worry creeps in, but I haven't stumbled into him.

Jace and I spend quite a bit of time together looking after Astrid. I'm still pumping, providing the hospital with breastmilk, and feeding her when she's hungry. She latches on and takes more than when she first started.

I swore I wouldn't bond with her, but it's impossible not to, staring down at the beautiful little girl nuzzled against my chest.

"Good news." The doctor heads toward us with a bright smile. "You'll be able to bring Astrid home tonight. She's been thriving and able to maintain her body temperature. She's gained a little weight too and doing well."

"That's great news," I whisper, staring down at Astrid.

But it doesn't feel great. It feels like another loss.

I don't want to be selfish. I went into this arrangement knowing that Jace would have a child, and we'd part ways. But even with all the money that he's offered me, after looking after Astrid and being with her every day in the hospital, she feels a bit like mine.

I'd never take her away from him. I'm not cut out to be a mother. I couldn't protect Austin. What makes me think I can protect Astrid?

Jace and the doctor discuss the specifics of Astrid's care. I zone out, not paying any attention as I focus on the little girl in my arms. I don't know how much more time we'll have together, and I want to savor every second.

———

Nightfall comes sooner than I'd like.

While I am relieved Astrid gets to go home with Jace, I worry about what life will be like for her. Will she have guards escorting her everywhere she goes as she grows up?

I'm not worried about the normalcy of her life. I knew from the beginning her father was a billionaire. Nothing will be normal for her. But I do wonder if she'll be a target of the other mafia family.

I don't want that life for her. But it's not my decision. And I have to make peace with how Jace chooses to raise her.

We head down to the lobby, Jace carrying the car seat with Astrid tucked inside, as we walk beside one another in silence.

A flurry of reporters rushes at us with cameras and microphones, their focus and attention on Jace.

"Jace, can you tell us if the rumors are true? Is the baby yours?" one reporter asks.

Heat flames over my cheeks. My stomach wrestles with survival. I raise my hand to cover my face and let my long hair help hide me from the cameras.

"What's the baby's name?" another reporter shouts. "Do you plan on marrying the mother and settling down from your bachelor lifestyle?"

Jace ignores them and rests a hand on my back, guiding me outside to an awaiting car. Matteo is in the driver's seat.

Jace opens the back door and gestures for me to get inside while he comes around the back of the vehicle and opens the opposite door, securing the car seat for Astrid.

A minute later, he's seated upfront with Matteo.

"What the hell was that?" I ask as we drive away from the hospital. I glance in the back window at the media frenzy we left behind.

"You weren't honestly thinking no one would find out that you gave birth to billionaire Jace Barone's child?" Matteo says. There's an air of defiance in his tone.

"I was hoping not to have my face plastered to the front-page news," I say. "Do they know that you're mafia?"

Matteo shoots Jace a glare.

"Relax, she knows to keep her mouth shut about the family. I'll deal with the media," Jace says.

"Right, like you dealt with them today," I mutter.

He ignored the reporters. If that was his way of dealing with the media, it didn't seem to work.

"Maybe you don't mind being hounded, but what happens when they track me down?" I ask.

He shifts in his seat and glances over his shoulder at me. "You'll remember to keep your mouth shut," Jace says.

"Is that a threat?"

"Consider it a warm suggestion," Jace says.

I have no intention of speaking to the press, but the nerve of him, to think that he can control what I say and do! When I return to the house, I'll pack my things and head out. I'm done with Jace Barone and his family.

Matteo clears his throat and reaches for a set of keys in the cupholder. He tosses them back at me. "We have an apartment lined up," Matteo says. "I already swept the place to make sure there weren't any bugs or other surveillance equipment."

While I'm still angry, I appreciate the little things, like privacy. "Thank you," I say. I don't plan on living under his roof forever. Even outside of his house, it's still one of Jace's properties. But I haven't spent time looking to rent an apartment or purchase a condo. And most places that I'd move into would require notice unless they have a vacancy.

Jace turns back around to face the front. "You are welcome to stay as long as you like."

I don't feel very invited by his body language. He's not so much as looking at me with his invitation. It feels like a formality. Well, don't worry, I won't accept. "That wasn't the agreement, Jace."

"I just thought if you're not ready to leave Astrid yet, you don't have to." Jace emits a soft sigh and glances at me briefly over his shoulder.

Astrid begins to fuss in the backseat as we come to a crawl from traffic.

"She's your daughter, not mine," I say.

He wanted this baby. He chose me as the surrogate. I only went along with it for the money. At least that's what it was about in the beginning, desperation. I also thought Luka had wanted me to agree to surrogacy to erase my debt.

A misunderstanding.

"Right," Jace says. There's a coldness and distance between us. It's time for me to go.

After a few minutes, Astrid's crying settles as we're moving through traffic.

———

I pack my belongings. I want to see Astrid, spend as much time with her as I can before I say goodbye, but the longer I hold her, the more it hurts to leave.

And I have to leave. This isn't my home, and Jace is a liar.

Should I take Astrid with me, far from the demons who chase after Jace?

If I do, his men will come after me.

Jace will hunt me down. He's a cold-blooded killer. Having murdered my husband and son, he could easily do it again.

But what kind of person am I if I leave her with a monster?

I don't bother to fold my clothes. I shove everything into the duffel bag. It's packed tight with maternity clothes. When I came to his house months ago, I had next to nothing. A car that was nearly out of gas that I was living out of. He turned my life around.

How can I ignore what he's done? The lies he's told, the truths that he's kept from me.

There are footsteps at the entrance to my bedroom. The door is open, and I glance over my shoulder.

It's Jace.

Astrid isn't in his arms.

"I put her in the crib. She's sound asleep from the drive," Jace says. "Are you all packed?"

"I think so," I say.

He steps into my room and grabs my bag, hauling it down the stairs and to my car, putting the duffel into the backseat.

Matteo steps out of the nearby office. "I texted you the address to the apartment complex where you'll be staying. Unless you want me to drive you over, make sure everything is safe?"

"I can handle it," I say.

Does that mean I'll no longer have Jace's men and guards following me? Does he think Luka is no longer a threat to me because we're not together?

I shouldn't stay in the city. I should get as far from Jace and Luka as possible. They will always be at war, and I don't want to be near the destruction they bring to the city or themselves.

I had dreams of leaving Los Angeles, traveling to Breckenridge for a fresh start.

Maybe it's time to make those dreams a reality.

Jace walks me outside and down to my car. He opens the driver's side door. Is he expecting a hug or kiss farewell?

Anger resonates through my body, pumping blood harder, making my heart race and my hands sweat.

"Take care of her, Jace," I say. "Luka's still out there, and he's dangerous."

His gaze tightens. "Not as dangerous as me."

Why does everything have to be a competition among men? I exhale a sigh. That's my cue to leave. I pull up the text from Matteo and grab directions to the apartment.

For tonight, I'll stay at the place he's arranged for me to live. But I can't stay there forever.

"Goodbye," I say and slip into the car.

He shuts the car door for me and steps out of the way. I fasten my seatbelt, start the engine, and head toward the iron gates. The guard opens the metal doors, allowing me to go.

It's the first time in months I've been allowed to leave alone.

It's refreshing and terrifying at the same time. I grip the steering wheel and follow the directions my phone gives as I head for my new apartment.

It's time to go home.

32

ONE WEEK LATER

JACE

I haven't heard from Olivia. She hasn't returned to work. Not that I expected her to, either.

I have Ryder, one of my best capos, keeping an eye on the apartment, alerting me to any visitors. Mainly, I'm keeping tabs to make sure Luka doesn't harass her. Not that I anticipate that he'll show up, but he did snatch her off the street while she was pregnant.

If he wants to hurt me, one way is through Olivia.

But if he assumes that we're broken up, then he should leave her alone. There's been no word from him.

It's been too silent.

Matteo has been keeping tabs on the Caruso family, ensuring that Luka isn't making another move on my family. He's managed, with a bit of help, to hack into their security and surveillance footage.

If they plan on coming after my family, we'll know about it.

Astrid cries a lot. It seems like she barely stops except to eat and sleep. I'm at wit's end on what to do, how to handle a shrieking infant.

Does she want her mother?

Olivia is gone. She's not coming back. And dare I say I miss her.

Cradling Astrid in my arms, the bottle at her lips, she doesn't take it. Her face is red, her cries growing louder.

"Might I make a suggestion, sir?" Matteo asks.

He must sense my frustration. He doesn't offer to hold Astrid. No one does. I don't know whether it's their fear of a newborn baby or they don't like kids. My men don't have children. They barely take care of themselves outside of the compound.

"What?" I snarl at him.

I'm exhausted and sleep-deprived. I don't know why I thought I could do this on my own.

"Ryder has reported to me that he hasn't seen Olivia leave her apartment a single time in the past week."

That doesn't sound right. "Did she have food or groceries brought in?"

Matteo's brow is furrowed. "No, sir. I'd like to have one of my men sent over to check on her well-being."

I cradle Astrid, rocking her in one arm when she finally takes the bottle. Overwhelming relief floods through me. "Fine, do it."

"Might I also make another suggestion?" Matteo asks.

I glare at him. "What now?" I'm grumpy as fuck, and he's not helping my mood.

"You need help with the little one. Might I suggest we bring in a nanny?"

"I don't want anyone else raising my child." The intention I had early on, before Olivia gave birth, had been ideal.

The reality is much different. How can we trust an outsider? I'm not interested unless the nanny is skilled in martial arts, weapons, and self-defense training. I don't want Mary Poppins watching my kid. I need someone with tactical expertise and private security training.

Which limits my search significantly.

And the thought of having a guard shadow the nanny, that's not an option. I can't risk anyone else knowing that we're mafia or that she too might end up in danger.

"Is this about Olivia, sir?" Matteo doesn't avoid the hard questions. It's what I pay him for, to be brutally honest. At the moment, it's not a quality I find endearing.

"No," I answer a little too quickly. Maybe I'm trying to convince myself it's not about her, either.

"Once we get into a routine, everything will be fine," I say, trying to reassure myself.

Astrid is wide awake. She's gotten into the habit of sleeping a few hours during the day and crying all hours of the night.

For the moment, she's quiet. She's fed, changed, and swaddled in a blanket in my arms. Her bright blue eyes stare up at me.

She has Olivia's eyes. Maybe they'll change when she gets older, but I doubt it. She also has wisps of strawberry blonde hair.

My stomach somersaults. In a way, I've taken two children from her.

No, Olivia left. She had to go to keep her safe. Plus, she was ready to leave. The agreement was complete, and her part was finalized.

But I was open to changing things. If only she hadn't looked at me with such disgust.

Am I the monster she believes me to be?

There's a soft knock on the nursery door.

I'm seated on a rocking chair near the window, with Astrid curled up in my arms.

Ryder pokes his head into the room, and his voice is soft and quiet as he speaks. "Sir."

"Come in," I say and nod for him to come closer. "Have you sent someone over to Olivia's apartment?" I want to know that everything is fine, but that would mean one of my men is incompetent, which doesn't bode well, either.

"Yes, I went myself to check on her."

"And?" I don't like being kept waiting.

Astrid begins to fuss in my arms, and I rock her against my chest, patting her back to settle her down. Not that it works.

The waterworks begin.

It's like she knows we're talking about her mother and isn't happy Olivia is gone.

Neither am I, but that's life.

I can't beg for Olivia to return to the compound. This isn't her life. She's not mine.

"She's not doing well, sir. My sister-in-law went through postpartum depression. I don't know much about it, but I worry she might be struggling with the same type of scenario."

That isn't what I wanted to hear. I hoped that she was doing well, happy to be on her own. "What do you suggest?" I ask.

"She probably needs to speak with a therapist of some kind, but I could be wrong. Perhaps you should visit her, see for yourself how she's doing."

Does she even want to see me? "I'm not sure that's a great idea," I say.

I want to see her, but I don't want to overstep. She's made it clear that she doesn't want to be with me and hates me for what I've done.

I don't blame her, but me showing up unannounced isn't going to brighten her mood.

"She refused to speak with me, slammed the door in my face," Ryder says.

"What makes you think she'll talk to me?"

"She said as much. Told me the only person she'll talk to is Don Barone."

Somehow, I doubt she used those words, called me don, but I don't question his tactics. He's trying to help, and Ryder freely refers to me as don, as I'm his boss.

33

OLIVIA

The apartment is dark. The curtains are closed, and I've yet to draw them. I don't want to seek sunlight or warmth. Any sort of happiness isn't for me.

Ryder showed up unannounced.

Is Jace checking up on me?

There'd be no other reason for one of his guards to visit me.

The place is a mess. I've been living out of my duffel bag. What's the point of unpacking it when I plan on leaving?

I lounge around in a pair of dark blue cargo pants and a long-sleeve t-shirt. I aim for comfort, but I don't feel the least bit content or relaxed.

There's a sharp knock at the door.

Is it Jace's men checking up on me again?

I wander through the darkened apartment. The lights are off, but it's morning. I could open a curtain for sunlight, but I don't.

"Just a second," I mutter to the person on the opposite side of the door. I make my way across the apartment, stumbling over my own feet but catching myself just before I hit the wooden door.

I curse under my breath and flip the lock, opening the door.

It's the last person in the world I want to see.

Luka Caruso.

I force the door shut, but he shoves his steel-toed boot inside, keeping the door ajar. He pushes me backward, knocking me to the ground.

I scramble to my feet, prepared to run to the bedroom, slam the door, and crawl through the fire escape exit.

But he has other ideas, and they don't involve my escape.

Luka grabs me by the hair and yanks me nice and close to his face. "Where's the baby?" He leers at me and drags me through the apartment, room by room.

"She's not here," I say.

Hasn't he figured it out by now?

Astrid was never mine.

I have no intention of telling Luka anything. I may despise what Jace did, but there's a darkness growing deep inside of me toward Luka.

Hatred.

It burns like a furnace on a deep winter's eve.

Scorching.

"Don Barone is a monster, keeping his child from her mother. I guess he was done with you after the baby was born," Luka says.

His breath stinks of onions and stale coffee.

My stomach roils at the stench. "Get off me!" I yank to pull away, but his fingers are still fisted in my long locks, and he isn't letting go.

"I made you an offer," Luka says. "You can still take it. I'll even up the ante. Five hundred thousand, and you get your little girl. All you have to do is take her and leave the country. Get far away from Don Barone, where he can't ever reach you."

"You'll want something in return." He's not offering me a cash payday without strings. I won't be his puppet.

"I want Jace to pay for what he did."

———

There's a firm knock on the door.

Luka is gone. He disappeared after roughing me up, leaving me with a bloody lip. I flip on the table side lamp and hesitantly approach the front door.

I glance through the peephole, this time being more careful about who I let into my apartment.

It's Jace, and he's holding Astrid in a sling wrapped around his chest.

I don't want to let him in, but are Luka's men nearby? It would be worse if they hurt Astrid. I could never live with myself if something happened to that little girl.

"What do you want, Jace?" I ask.

"Let me inside."

I shuffle my feet and relent, unlocking the door. He'd never hurt me. At least not physically. I unclasp the lock and take a step back. "It's open." I turn and head for the kitchen so he can't see my bloodied lip. I cleaned it up, but it's swollen and bruised.

I reach for a glass from the cabinet and turn on the tap, grabbing something to drink—a distraction.

He closes the door and secures the lock. I hear it click into place. I pause in the kitchen, my back still to him.

"How are you doing?" Jace asks like it's the most ordinary question and we're at work. His demeanor is friendly, warm, and not the least bit professional.

He's casual, like we're old friends, and he's just stopping by to see me.

"I'm fine." I sip the water as I stand over the sink.

Jace comes into the kitchen. He's quiet, methodical. He opens the fridge.

"Help yourself," I mutter.

"To what? It's empty."

"There are a few things in there," I stammer. It's not exactly empty. I haven't starved myself for the past week since I left, but it's not like I've eaten great, either. There were a few food items that Matteo must have put into the freezer, which I thawed and cooked for dinner.

"One meal a day isn't enough, Olivia."

I spin around on my heels to face him. "Why do you care?" I ask. I want to stare at him, shout, and remind him that he's the bad guy. Not me.

But one glance at Astrid curled up against his chest, and my heart breaks. My bottom lip trembles and my eyes burn with tears.

I rush past him, making a beeline for the bathroom to run and hide.

Jace grabs me by the arm, stopping me from fleeing.

"What happened to your lip?"

"I walked into the door."

He doesn't buy my excuse. "No, if you had that yesterday when Ryder stopped by, he would have told me. What happened?" Jace isn't the least bit calm or collected. His anger is bubbling to the surface.

"It doesn't concern you," I say. "I'm not your problem anymore."

"Is that what you think you are to me, a problem?" Jace scoffs. He lets go of my arm, but I don't run.

What's the point? He's not going to hurt me. Not like Luka would when he showed up, which still leaves a rock in the pit of my stomach. A heavy ache that torments me.

Luka instructed that I take Astrid and leave the country.

It wasn't a suggestion.

But I can't tell Jace about what happened, not at the apartment. What if the place is bugged like the last time?

"I want you to take me home," I say.

His brow knits, confused. "Okay. Back to the compound?" He doesn't put up the slightest bit of a fight.

"Yes," I say. I'll tell him everything when we're inside and where I know it's safe.

He grabs my hand and pulls me close. Astrid is nestled between us, tucked snuggly against his chest. His lips capture mine in a searing hot kiss.

"I love you," he whispers, pulling back, staring deep into my gaze.

My heart pitter-patters in my chest. I'm not going back to the compound to be with him. I'm going back to protect him and Astrid.

And I'll tell him, but not here, not where Luka could be listening in or watching us. I have to tread carefully.

His thumb grazes over the injury to my lips. His eyes flicker with something unfamiliar that I've never seen before.

Is it rage?

"Let's get your things, and you'll come home with me," Jace says.

The car ride to the compound is met with silence.

Astrid is buckled into the backseat and sound asleep in her car seat.

I honestly don't know what to say. While I doubt Luka is eavesdropping in the car, I don't have the strength to tell Jace everything, like I thought I would.

Silence is easier. I can't disappoint him if I don't speak.

I stare out the passenger window, and my eyes lazily shut after a few minutes. I'm tired. The day is dreary, which matches my mood.

Jace gently caresses my cheek with his warm fingers. "Hey, sleepyhead. We're here."

"Thanks," I mumble and open my eyes to wake up further. I unclasp my seatbelt and climb out of the car.

Jace grabs the car seat carrier and brings Astrid inside with us. She's still sound asleep. I step inside the foyer, the compound entirely too familiar. I spent weeks under the roof, mostly in my room, while pregnant. Not that it wasn't a nice room, furnished and quite comfortable. But I didn't ever think I'd be back here. Let alone asking Jace to bring me here.

"Home sweet home?" he asks with a warm smile. He puts the car seat carrier down and removes his coat and shoes.

I unzip my jacket. I don't intend on staying for long, but I need a few minutes of his time and the strength not to falter.

He tosses his car keys to Vincent. "Grab Olivia's duffel bag out of the trunk, will you?"

Vincent hurries outside into the cold without a coat or gloves.

"Can we talk?" I ask.

Jace nods, and his eyes crinkle with a hint of a smile. Like he thinks he knows what this conversation is about.

Except he doesn't know. He couldn't know that Luka had come by and threatened my family.

They are my family, even if we're not together. I'm still connected to Jace and Astrid. They'll always hold a place inside my heart.

"Sure, how about we head upstairs to the nursery? We can put Astrid down and talk."

He carries the car seat with Astrid nestled asleep inside up the stairs. I follow just a few short steps behind him.

I should have told him the truth in the car. Waiting is going to make it worse. It's like a band-aid that needs to be ripped off fast to make it painless.

He leads me down the hall to his room. He opens the door, letting me inside. His scent is overwhelming, permeating every inch of his bedroom. In the corner beside the bed is a bassinet for Astrid.

"The nursery is just through this door," he says, leading me through the adjoining room and into Astrid's bedroom.

Inside, there's a crib, changing table, and a rocking chair near the window. I've seen the nursery a few times, but only while I was pregnant. I'd never gone through Jace's room to enter, either.

He places the car seat on the floor and bends down, unbuckling Astrid from the seat.

She stirs as he guides her out of the seat and around the buckle. Her cheeks redden, and I'm waiting for the sudden wail of a crying infant.

I'm not mistaken. Astrid has a set of lungs on her that can probably be heard through the entire compound.

That girl can cry and wake the dead.

Jace groans and lifts her to his chest, bouncing her in his arms, trying to calm her down. "Shh," he says, attempting to soothe Astrid. "It's okay. I've got you."

Her cheeks are red as she screams her discontent.

I watch from across the room. It's not my place to intervene. Astrid is his daughter. She's no longer mine.

"Shit," I curse, realizing I'm leaking breastmilk through my t-shirt. "Do you mind if I—"

"You want to feed her?" Jace asks, his eyes wide, filled with hope.

I was asking if I could borrow a shirt, but he's practically handing over Astrid to me. His arms are outstretched for me to take the weeping baby.

Cradling Astrid into my arms, I carry her over to the rocking chair and sit. My t-shirt is soaked, so I remove it and toss it to the floor. It's not like Jace hasn't seen me breastfeed before. Astrid is still wailing her highest pitch imaginable until I finally get situated and her to latch on.

How do I tell Jace that I'm not back for good? That I only suggested that I come here because I needed to warn him about Luka?

Staring down at Astrid, I don't want to leave. This is exactly where I should be, with her.

But what about Jace?

34

JACE

I've made mistakes. I'm not an innocent man, but I'd never knowingly hurt Astrid or Olivia.

I'll give Olivia as much time as she needs to realize that I want what's best for her. She's back in my life, back at the compound, but she's slightly withdrawn. I've considered that it's probably her hormones. She gave birth a few weeks ago and leaving Astrid couldn't have been easy.

I knew they bonded, and I should have been more adamant about Olivia staying at the compound, or at least being an essential part of Astrid's life.

I bring Olivia a dry t-shirt, one of mine that she can wear as she finishes feeding Astrid and puts her down in the crib for a nap.

"Thanks," she says and pulls it on over her head.

"You wanted to talk?"

She chews on her bottom lip and avoids eye contact. "Yeah," she whispers.

I reach out, my thumb grazing the gash on her lips. "What happened?" I want the truth.

"Luka," she whispers, staring down at the ground.

"He showed up at the apartment?" I ask. I'll have to have a word with Ryder. He never mentioned that Luka stopped by her place. "When?"

"A couple of hours before you showed up today," Olivia whispers.

I swallow the lump forming in my throat. I'm afraid to ask, but I need the truth. "What did he want?"

"What doesn't he want when it comes to making your life hell?" Olivia says. "He wants to separate you from Astrid."

I shouldn't be surprised, but I'm unsettled by the fact he showed up to give Olivia a message. There's something off about all of it. I gently let my thumb graze over the damage to her lip. "I don't like that he roughed you up in the process of threatening me," I say.

"I should have done a better job of protecting myself," Olivia whispers, her gaze locked on mine.

"No." I won't let her take the blame for the monster who is Luka Caruso. "This is in no way your fault. There should have been a guard stationed outside your apartment." I neglect to mention the surveillance footage, which must have been tampered with if Ryder wasn't alerted to the visit.

I want to double-check the footage. I need to know without a doubt that Ryder isn't working for Luka and ignored the attack. While I trust my men, I always have to be careful to make sure I'm not naïve and stupid, either. I had Markus investigated after Olivia's abduction. He was clean, but is Ryder?

"I've got a couple of things to do while Astrid is napping," I say.

"Do you mind if I stay in here with Astrid?" She glances over at the crib like she doesn't want to part with the sleeping infant.

"Sure, if you get tired, feel free to lie down in my room." I point toward the adjoining door.

We haven't worked out sleeping arrangements. Are we together, or am I getting my hopes up for no reason at all?

I leave her alone in the nursery with Astrid and quietly slip out into the adjoining room and then the main door, to keep from waking my daughter.

I head down the stairs to my office, wanting to see the surveillance footage for myself. There weren't any cameras inside her apartment. I didn't want to spy on her, but outside the main door of her apartment was in no way off-limits.

It's my building. I own the damn place.

I flip on the light in the office. The room is quite chilly, and I sit in the cold leather chair. I haven't been in here in quite some time. I've neglected my work duties for raising a child.

Eventually, I'll get back to it when things settle down. I should consider hiring a nanny to help with Astrid, but the thought of a stranger looking after my baby girl tears me up inside.

"Sir," Matteo says, as he pokes his head into the office. "Do you have a minute?"

"Come in and shut the door, would you?"

Matteo does as asked. He's carrying several sheets of paper, printouts of something. I can't be bothered to focus on the business—the mafia or Barone Industries at the moment. My attention is entirely on Olivia and Luka.

My family.

I flip on my laptop and punch in my password, waiting for the machine to boot.

"What's that?" I ask, seeing the stack of pages he's printed. It's copies of something, but what is it that he needs to show me?

"I'm glad you're sitting down," Matteo says.

"I don't like the sound of that," I grumble under my breath.

There's static crackling through the room, and I glance to my right.

On top of the dark green filing cabinet is the baby monitor. It's on and transmitting from the nursery. I left it plugged in and forgot about the damn unit. It's not like I've left Astrid alone for more than five minutes. Even when she's sleeping, I usually have her at my side, or she's cuddled against my chest.

"I wish I knew what to do." Olivia's voice carries through the baby monitor.

"I swear if she wakes Astrid," I mutter.

Matteo holds up a hand for me to wait. "I think you should listen," he says and steps closer to the monitor, turning it up.

"You want me to spy on the mother of my child?"

Has he lost his mind?

I may not have gotten much sleep recently, especially with Astrid now at home, but Matteo has been handling the business. "Is the job too much for you?" I ask.

His gaze tightens, and his jaw is tight. He slams the papers on my desk, letting me see whatever it is that has him in a tizzy. "Your girl—Olivia, whatever the hell she is, she's playing you."

I don't believe him.

I glance down at the bank receipts. There's a deposit into her account for five hundred thousand dollars, and it's not from me.

"Did you trace the account that deposited the funds?" I ask. He can't give me bits and pieces without having an explanation already in mind.

"Yes, and it goes to a shell corporation. When I dug a little deeper, I was able to pinpoint it to Luka Caruso. Sir, she's playing you."

I don't believe it.

I can't believe it.

"She wouldn't do that," I say, staring down at the evidence. Is that why she wanted to be brought back to the compound, to kidnap my daughter?

"She would, and she did. She also booked two plane tickets to the Maldives." He shows me a copy of the receipt for the nonrefundable flight scheduled to leave tomorrow.

"The Maldives? There are extradition laws," I say. She can't just steal my daughter and run away.

"Not with the Maldives, and in parental custody cases, even most countries that do allow for extradition don't always follow through."

While she doesn't have a passport for Astrid, it wouldn't be hard to have one faked, especially by a scumbag like Don Caruso. If he's helping her flee the country, then he probably has the paperwork she needs to leave.

Olivia's voice carries through the baby monitor into my office. "All I want is to protect you," she whispers. "How can I do that with two mafia families fighting over you?"

"I want security around the compound increased. Every soldier and capo, have him brought back here to make sure Olivia doesn't kidnap my daughter."

I don't bother looking at the footage that I came into my office to view. It doesn't matter. It's irrelevant now that I've seen the truth and heard enough on the monitor to confirm my suspicions.

I stand. My chair squeaks as it slides against the wood floor behind me. "Have the alarm armed and two of my men stationed outside the nursery. I want two additional men following Olivia anywhere she goes. If she goes to the bathroom across the hall, I want to know about it."

I grab the papers in my fist, the pages crinkling as I storm out of my office and up the stairs. The last thing I want is to wake Astrid, but I need answers from Olivia, and I'm not sure I'm going to like what she says.

35

OLIVIA

Astrid is sound asleep.

Her tiny arms and legs kick every so often while in slumber. I stand over her crib, watching her movements. She's perfect.

"Step away from the crib," Jace commands as he enters through the nursery door.

Markus and Vincent stand at the entrance to Jace's bedroom. Vincent's hand is on his holster at his hip. Behind Jace are Matteo and Ryder.

"What is going on?" I whisper, glancing from the other men back to Jace.

He's holding several sheets of paper, printouts of something that has him rattled.

"Did Luka threaten you?" I ask. I wouldn't put it past the mobster after he showed up earlier today at my apartment.

Jace scoffs under his breath and grabs me by the arm, dragging me forcefully out of the nursery.

"Where are we going?" I ask, shrugging out of his grasp.

He's strong, his grip tight as he leads me down the hallway.

"I should put you in the basement prison." His voice holds no hint of mercy or kindness. "But I won't." He drags me down to his office and slams the door shut. Through the frosted glass, I can see men standing on the opposite side.

But we're alone.

The slight crackle of the baby monitor echoes through the room when Astrid whimpers in sleep.

"I don't know what you think you heard," I say, glancing from the baby monitor to him.

Did I say something that I shouldn't have about Luka's threats? I can't even remember what I said two minutes earlier. My brain is in a fog. Fear grips me.

He tosses the pages of documents, printouts of some type of documentation all across his oak desk.

"Quit lying to me," he steps closer, invading my personal space. His stone gaze pierces through me. "How long have you been working with Luka? Since the beginning?"

He already knew that Luka threatened me and forced my hand to get information on the flash drive.

"What are you talking about?" I ask, not understanding his anger toward me. "I don't work for Luka or with him. He's a monster."

"Is that right? You only take money from him. Five hundred thousand dollars' worth of money," Jace says. He points at the pages on the desk, tapping on the sheet of paper as proof.

"It's not true. The only money I've received is from you."

"Don't lie to me. I've seen the statement, the transactions, the paper trail. You even have two plane tickets to the Maldives for tomorrow night."

What is he talking about? Luka didn't even tell me about the plane tickets. "It has to be a setup," I say, rationalizing what he's seen. "I didn't take money from Caruso."

"Right, it just happened to land in your account. Don't you get it, Olivia? He owns you. Taking money from the mafia, it doesn't come without hoops to jump through and a thousand strings attached."

I fold my arms across my chest defensively. "I haven't looked at my checking account today. Luka did it to set me up. He wants me to take Astrid and flee the country."

"So, you admit to making plans and kidnapping my daughter?"

"What? Of course not! I didn't book any plane tickets, and I certainly don't recognize the payment. If the money is really in the account, then he's to blame."

Could this all be a complete misunderstanding?

I shove my hand into my pants pocket for my cell phone.

Jace hovers and watches my every move as I unlock my phone, open the app for my bank, and review my checking account balance.

"He must have hacked my account," I say, glancing at Jace.

I can't deny the lump-sum payment or the deduction for the airline, neither of which I did.

"That's convenient," Jace growls. He pins me with his stare. "You should know, I'm not letting you kidnap my daughter. I've secured the compound with additional guards and will have men watching your every move."

I'd expect nothing less from a mafia don.

"Luka wants this to tear us apart, make sure that you don't trust me. He's rattling you," I say, trying to reason with him. "He wants revenge for you killing his father."

"And what about you?" He tilts his head, his gaze never leaving mine. "Is that what you want, revenge? A child for a child."

"I want my son back, but I know that isn't an option. And unlike you, Jace, I'm not a monster. I wouldn't hurt Astrid."

I should blame Jace. After all, he's the responsible party for destroying my life and murdering my family. Austin and John are dead because of the fire that he ordered. But my marriage with John wasn't perfect. It wasn't anything close to ideal. I loved Austin, though.

"I didn't mean to hurt your family," Jace says. "They were a casualty of war."

Easy for him to say. "A war that my family should never have been a part of," I remind him. "How can you promise to keep Astrid safe when you're still fighting with Don Caruso? He won't ever stop chasing after you."

It's not that I want to tear Astrid away from her father. It's that I want to keep her safe. Fleeing to a foreign country, moving halfway across the world, where I'll be isolated from the few people who I know, it's not what I want.

And if Luka continues to threaten us, what other choice is there?

"You're right. I have to put an end to his reign," Jace says.

"How do you plan on doing that?" I ask.

He brushes past me, ignoring my question. Jace opens the office door, four of his men stand at the entrance to the office, awaiting his orders.

"Markus and Vincent, I want you both guarding Olivia. Matteo, get the Capos brought down to the war room and the soldiers ready. We're going to war."

"What?" I shriek.

Did I hear him correctly?

"Jace, no. This is what he wants. He had to suspect that you'd investigate my financial records. Why else purchase plane tickets?"

"Take her upstairs," Jace orders one of his men. "And grab her phone. I don't want any loose ends or leaks."

Markus grabs my arm and pulls me away from Jace, leading me back up the stairwell. He snatches my cell phone, shoving it into his pocket.

Jace and several of his men pile into another room down the hallway, slamming the door behind themselves.

I shiver and yank my arm out of Markus' grip. "You don't have to manhandle me. I can walk up the stairs myself."

He leads me into Jace's bedroom. "We'll be outside your door," Markus says, warning me that if I try to leave, I won't get far.

"Right."

Where would I go? Men like Jace and Luka have infinite resources to track me down.

At least there isn't a guard blocking my way into the nursery. I check on Astrid. She's thankfully still sound asleep. I shut off the baby monitor, unplug it, and open the door, tossing it into the hallway with a loud thud.

I shut the door before Markus or Vincent can object.

Astrid wiggles in her crib, her eyes closed, her feet kicking every so often in her sleep. I watch her, careful not to make a sound as she sleeps, oblivious to the dangers lurking all around her.

I won't take her from her father. I'm not the monster. Besides, there's nowhere that I could go where Jace couldn't track me down and find me. He's made that clear, investigating my finances.

I should be angry with him for betraying my trust. But I'm not. My stomach tenses and bubbles with anxiety. I quietly retreat from the crib and climb into Jace's bed.

His scent is all over the sheets, the bed, even the room. I shut my eyes as I rest my head on the pillow. I'm used to hiding from myself, my pain, and the world around me.

Just as I begin to drift off to sleep, Astrid awakens. Her cries are high-pitched, and I doubt she'll fall back asleep anytime soon.

I shuffle out of bed and into the nursery, lifting Astrid into my arms. I bring her over to the changing table to change her diaper, which seems to do the trick.

Her blue eyes are glistening with tears, and her cheeks are flushed from crying. I drop a quick kiss to her nose. "I know, babe. I'm worried about him too."

Maybe I should be angry with Jace, hate him for what he's done, destroying my family. But I don't hate him.

I feel sorry for Jace. Living in the shadows as a don with the spotlight on him as a billionaire. It's not an easy life to have enemies at every turn, always having to watch his back.

There's a strange sense of comfort in knowing that if the tragedies hadn't taken place, Astrid wouldn't be here in my arms. Those moments led me here, with her.

Astrid gurgles and coos, reaching out for my finger. She's perfect. Everything about her, except her father runs the mafia.

36

JACE

"They'll be expecting us," I say to Matteo as we study the blueprints for the Caruso complex.

"Yes, but my source tells me they have a dog fight scheduled for midnight, off-site. Luka isn't likely to attend. His second and a dozen of his men will be taking bets and monitoring the crowd. It should give us the advantage if we wait until his men leave the compound."

I hope he's right. I've never known Luka to be into dogfighting, but anything that involves a glorious payday and illegal activities, he's interested in investing in.

"I don't want to leave our compound weak. We still have my daughter upstairs," I remind Matteo and the capos. We need to make sure this place is a fortress before we strike an attack.

"We could put your family into one of the prison cells. The walls are impenetrable, and if you have the key, no one else could get to them," Ryder says.

He's one of the youngest capos who has worked his way up the ladder in a short time. He's also an idiot if he thinks I'm putting my newborn daughter inside a metal cage.

"I ought to shoot you for that suggestion," I say, glaring at Ryder.

Imprisoning my family isn't an option to keep them safe. Being locked inside the compound ought to keep them protected.

"My apologies, Don Barone," Ryder says, quick to apologize for his brash and stupid comment.

I ignore his eagerness. He's young. Foolish. And he is probably looking to further his career. If he's not careful, he'll end up dead tonight.

Matteo clears his throat. "You have two of the most experienced guards looking after your daughter, sir. I assure you that even with our soldiers making an attack, the house will be impenetrable."

"You're willing to risk your life on that promise?" I ask, meeting Matteo's stare.

I trust the man, but if my family ends up dead, someone will have to pay. I want to know that without a doubt, when I leave to order the hit on Luka, my family at the compound remains safe and out of harm's way.

His eyes flinch before he speaks.

Even Matteo realizes it's not a promise that he can guarantee.

"That's what I thought. I want the guards doubled upstairs, outside the nursery. Four men are making sure my daughter is safe."

"And what about your—Olivia?" Matteo asks.

"She is under my protection as long as she follows the rules. The minute she puts Astrid in harm's way, kill her."

I don't fuck around.

Do I care about Olivia?

Significantly, but I'm not about to risk my daughter's life to a woman who could betray me. She hasn't proven to me beyond a doubt that she is trustworthy. It's why I had her phone removed from her possession. I don't trust that she won't reach out to Luka and warn him that we're coming.

"Yes, sir." Matteo doesn't argue because he knows that I'm right.

———

I don't say goodbye. Not to Astrid, and certainly not to Olivia.

Saying goodbye means that I may not make it back.

That's not an option because my daughter needs me. I'm her father.

We surround Caruso's compound as best we can. It's on the water, which means we have to make sure he can't flee on his boat.

Matteo heads around back with six soldiers. They have orders to light the boat on fire, but not before we breach the walls and enter the complex.

We don't want to alert him that we're coming.

There are dozens of guards around the entire property.

We brought more. As far as I can tell, they're outmatched and outnumbered, and we have the element of surprise.

But they know the layout of the facility. Our blueprints are originals from the construction of the building. We can't say for sure that any changes that were made are accounted for or if there's a safe room.

Luka doesn't seem the kind of man to cower and hide in a firefight. But some men are afraid of death as it stalks close.

Not me.

I've seen death.

I've fought it and won. Will I be so lucky again tonight?

I glance down at my watch. It's two minutes to midnight. My men are in position. A significant number of guards already abandoned their posts for the dog fight, but there are still eight men I count outside the walls, watching the perimeter.

We have to move silently. Any chance that they spot us or hear our weapons and Luka will flee. If not in his boat, then in one of his vehicles.

I have men securing the perimeter, setting explosives around multiple exits, wired by a detonator.

My soldiers have trained for this battle. We've waited for this day to come, to take out Don Caruso.

My earpiece is secure.

"Sir, we have movement in the back corridor," Matteo says to the group.

Is Luka on to us? Did he get wind of our arrival?

"What kind of movement?" I ask, careful to keep my voice down and from traveling far.

Two guards are pacing the perimeter outside. They have semiautomatic weapons in hand, but their fingers aren't on the trigger. They don't appear to have sensed us yet. Or if they have, they're pretending not to be aware of our arrival.

I wouldn't put it past Luka to run and not warn his men.

He's a coward.

"Is it Don Caruso?" I ask.

"Unconfirmed," Matteo says.

There's a beat before he answers. I presume he's staring through night vision goggles, waiting for the right moment to get a glimpse of the man at the back entrance.

"Negative. It's a guard outside for a cigarette break," Matteo says.

It couldn't be that easy to kill the man in his backyard.

"The alarm's been deactivated," Bryce says into the earpiece.

That's our signal that it's time to move at my command.

If I hadn't been on the scene, Matteo would be giving the orders. But I need to see this mission through and be confident that Don Caruso is dead.

I give the command, and the soldiers launch forward, quietly moving along the perimeter, taking out the guards on the outside, protecting the complex.

We breach the entrance. It isn't hard with their numbers down, the dog fight commencing across town at an old warehouse Caruso owns. My phone is on silent, but my men know to reach me if there is any suspicious activity or movement on our compound.

Thankfully, all is silent.

But the silence can only last so long. We sneak in through the front door, uninvited. From the opposite end of the building, there's a rash of gunfire that erupts, sending our mission from silent to deadly.

Not just deadly for Caruso's men, but ours as well.

I direct half of the soldiers with me to head toward the gunfire and protect our men. The other half follows as we sweep the first floor, room by room, taking out anyone who stands in our way with a weapon.

There are casualties of war. Luka has no family, no wife or children that I worry about endangering. But that doesn't mean there aren't innocent people forced by his hand beneath this roof. He dabbles in many illicit and illegal ventures, whether any of them involve women or children, I don't know.

I can't let rational thought dictate my commands.

Luka is a monster who must be stopped. "This way," I order my soldiers to follow me up the stairs.

There's no sign of Don Caruso on the first floor.

We will find him, and he'll be forced to pay for his sins when we do. His death will be swift, and while it would give me pleasure torturing the bastard who has been tormenting my family, most of all, I want him dead.

Several guards are at the top of the landing, waiting for us.

We shoot to kill. Aiming from one man to the next. The guards aren't wearing any type of Kevlar, and they don't have semi-automatic weapons as we attack. It makes the shoot an easier kill.

They weren't expecting us.

Good.

Before we breach the second floor, I reload my gun, sweeping room by room for guards or anyone armed with a weapon. While our goal is to take out Don Caruso, anyone who stands in our way is a threat.

The rooms on the second floor are empty as we check the closets, under the bed, the bathrooms, and behind the shower curtain, anywhere that a coward like Caruso might hide.

On to the next room.

As we reach the final door near the second set of stairs that go back down, I lead the way inside.

A canister of CS gas is tossed at us, filling the room and permeating out into the hallway with the door left ajar.

Gunfire erupts from all directions. I can't see the men, but flashes from their muzzles and the sound of gunfire gives me the general direction.

The smoke is just that, like a fog that wafts over the room. It's slightly uncomfortable, but manageable. My men and I have built up a tolerance to repeated exposure in training my soldiers.

Two walls are covered, the third is empty.

We move fast along the third wall, shooting at the intended targets through a blanket of smoke that provides cover as we narrow in on Don Caruso. He must be here, holed up with his guards, probably cowering in the corner.

Two of my men take a bullet, one to the chest, the other to the shoulder.

It's dangerous, the closer we get, but it doesn't stop or slow me down. There's no thought, just action.

Several bullets come at me. One grazes my leg. It's a horrible shot if they intend to kill me.

I power through the pain and take out three guards. The closer I get, I can see their faces, the masks covering them from the gas.

I rip off one of the masks, forcing him to breathe in the obnoxious fumes and grip the barrel of his gun, pointing it up toward the ceiling and slamming the guard in the face with his weapon.

He coughs and wheezes from the smoke plume, and his nose drips blood from the blow to his face. It doesn't take much for me to knock him on his ass with my fists, two blows to the face, and he's stumbling around before his knees buckle and give way.

My men disarm two additional guards during the fight, and behind me is the distant sound of footsteps.

Reinforcements.

Are they Caruso's men or mine?

"Matteo, talk to me. I'm on the second floor, back stairwell, last room," I say, waiting to hear from them via the earpiece.

It's been radio silent for a while. Too long for my liking.

Did his men stop Matteo and the soldiers at the rear entrance? There'd been a firefight, but I'd sent additional units to help.

Was it not enough?

Luka is in the corner, behind the last two guards protecting him.

They fall, but it isn't over.

Gunfire erupts from behind us, taking out my guards. Caruso shoots at us from the opposite side.

The smoke is a thin haze, allowing me to see the men with guns shooting at us.

A dozen soldiers are armed with their guns pointed at us. The reinforcements aren't my men.

Static crackles through the earpiece.

Are they jamming our signal, or did they kill every one of my men?

"Surrender, and I'll let you live," Luka shouts across the room at me. He takes several long strides toward me.

There's nowhere for me to go. If I shoot Luka, I die.

His gun is aimed at my head, the safety off, and a dozen other soldiers have their weapons pointed at me.

Fuck.

"What's it going to be, Jace?" Luka asks.

I'm stalling. Hopefully, it won't end in my death. "How about we make a deal?"

Luka's laugh is dark and sinister. "Do you think you have something worth bargaining for?" He shakes his head, glancing me over. "There's nothing you can offer me that I want. You murdered my father. I want you dead."

"Word on the street is you didn't even like your old man."

"What? Do you expect a thank you for killing him and allowing me to run the city?" Luka asks. He's silent for a second. A dark smirk crosses his features. "There is something I want, and maybe I'll let your little girl live. You, on the other hand, I'm prepared to bury."

"You won't touch my daughter," I seethe, my top lip snarling in disgust.

Luka shrugs. "Or what, you'll kill me? You'll be dead, old man." He chuckles and shakes his head, keeping the gun poised at my temple. "Better yet, I bring that tight girlfriend of yours into my home, fuck her like she deserves from a real man, and give her the family that you can't. The one that you stole from her."

My mouth goes dry. I stare into his cold gaze, daring him to kill me. To end my suffering.

Gunfire erupts from behind the soldiers.

Static crackles through the earpiece again. "Boss, we've got your back," Matteo says.

I've never been so happy to hear his voice in my life.

The guards turn toward the approaching gunfire, protecting their don, leaving him vulnerable to me.

It's Luka versus me. But it feels like I'm fighting the world for survival. If Luka wins, my family is in danger. Not just my mafia family, but Astrid and Olivia.

I refuse to go down without a fight.

"You'll leave my family alone!" I yank the barrel of the gun upwards and away from his grasp.

His knee smashes up into my groin, causing me to see stars. The bullet graze hurt, but this is crueler.

My stomach roils, but I keep fighting and swallow the pain and keep my head held high. I slam my fist up into his face, knocking him backward.

Don Caruso stumbles but catches himself. He's not going down that easily, but he's dropped the gun, and it's slid across the floor. He's a trained fighter. It comes with the territory of being part of the mafia.

"I'm going to make your whore my wife," Luka threatens, lowering his head and barreling into my chest, knocking me backward into the wall.

I grab Luka by the hair, ripping him away from my body before kneeing him in the groin and kicking him in the stomach as he's doubled over. He drops to the ground, reaching for the abandoned gun on the floor.

Shit.

I dive for the weapon, but I'm too late.

He's quicker, spins around on the floor, and points the barrel up at me, finger on the trigger.

Bang!

Pain sears through me before I crumble to the floor.

Darkness.

37

OLIVIA

Astrid is fast asleep in her bassinet beside the bed.

There's a commotion outside the door and voices downstairs. It's not just chatter amongst the men watching over me.

What's going on?

I'm quiet, my footsteps silent as I head for the door. I need to know if we're in danger. Is Astrid safe?

What about Jace and his men?

The minute I open the door, Markus folds his arms across his chest and glares. "Go back to bed."

It's well past two in the morning, but I don't care. I can't sleep. "What's going on?" I ask. It's hard to sleep through the racket downstairs, let alone the fact Jace is on a mission to stop Don Caruso.

When isn't he on a mission to kill that lowlife? "Is Jace back?"

Markus glances from me to Vincent. Those two have been pretty close lately, guarding my ass at every turn.

"What aren't you telling me?" I can feel the heaviness of their silence, and it makes my stomach sink.

"Jace is downstairs, but he's been shot," Markus says.

At least he has the integrity to tell me the truth. "What do you mean, Jace has been shot? Why isn't he at the hospital?"

"That isn't an option," Vincent says and clears his throat. "Get back in your room."

"No," I say defiantly and fold my arms across my chest. "I want to see Jace."

"Unless you know how to do surgery to remove a bullet and stitch a man up, get back in your room," Vincent barks orders at me.

I never did like Vincent. Markus, at least, is pleasant enough to be around. My gaze tightens, and I chew on my bottom lip. There's no chance of me sneaking past the guards with Markus and Vincent beside the door, and two more men are outside the nursery door.

"Get back in your room and go to bed," Markus says.

"But what about Jace?" I ask.

How can they expect me to sleep knowing that he's injured and his life is on the line?

Vincent opens the bedroom door and shoves me inside, shutting the door behind me.

"Asshole," I mutter.

There isn't much for me to do but wait it out.

What about Luka? Is he still alive out there? Will he retaliate?

———

I barely sleep all night, and when the bedroom door handle turns and the lock clicks, I sit straight up.

"Jace?"

I breathe a sigh of relief when he stumbles into the bedroom. The curtains are shut, but there's light peeking through the shades.

Glancing at the clock, it's nearly eleven in the morning. I did fall asleep sometime rather late or early this morning.

He's barefoot, his shirt removed, his chest bare but bandaged over his shoulder.

I climb out of bed, wanting to see him, touch him, and know that this isn't a dream.

"I'm fine," he says through gritted teeth.

"Yeah, you look fine." He looks like hell, but I don't say it. At least not in so many words.

His hair is disheveled. There's a smear of blood across his cheek. His pants are the only thing that looks normal on him. The black slacks make it difficult to see if there are bloodstains but they are torn.

The blood on his cheek, is it his or someone else's?

"What happened?" I ask.

I need to know if it's over. If Astrid and I are no longer in danger. But can it ever really be over? Even if Luka is dead, won't there be another snake to rise and take his place?

The man had quite a number of associates. It's no secret he threatens the city.

"We went in and attacked their compound," Jace says.

His eyes are listless as he avoids my stare.

I climb off the mattress and stand in front of him, blocking his path. He has to tell me more. Are we safe?

"What happened in there?" I ask. "Your men, they wouldn't tell me anything."

His words hold no hint of emotion. "Good."

"Good? Jace, what's going on? Is Luka dead?" I've never wanted someone murdered so much in my life. Killing is wrong. Death is final. But somehow, ending Luka's life is the kind of closure that I need.

"His head is downstairs if you want to see for yourself."

I stumble back onto the bed.

I gasp at his bluntness. He's always been brazen, but this is something else.

Darker. Rougher. Less refined. "Please, tell me you don't mean that," I say.

"My men killed the bastard who's been threatening my daughter and you." Jace heads for the bathroom.

"Where are you going?"

"To take a shower," he grunts.

Doesn't he know anything about wounds and healing? "You can't with the bandage. You're going to have to keep the wound dry and clean. It needs time to heal."

"Don't tell me what I can and can't do," he snaps.

I take a sharp breath in as he storms into the bathroom and slams the door—the pictures on the wall rattle.

Astrid wails, awaking from slumber.

38

JACE

I step under the hot shower, the spray at my back, letting the water run down my body.

I hate that Olivia is right. I know how to take care of a fresh wound. Does she think this is the first time I've been shot?

It's not and likely won't be the last.

I tip my head back, letting the water soak through my hair. I'm quick to shower, but mostly I just needed the time alone.

Olivia invades every waking thought. Even when the physician downstairs heavily sedated me, I was dreaming about her.

I dry off, the bandage dry except for the moisture in the air, making it a bit humid. Thankfully, the doctor used a waterproof dressing on the wound.

I didn't bring any clothes into the bathroom. I don't usually when I shower, but I'm also not accustomed to sharing my bedroom with anyone.

I wrap the towel around my waist and step out of the bathroom. The hot steam follows behind me.

The medication the doctor gave has helped dull the pain and probably a few of my senses.

Olivia is stretched out on the mattress, her legs buried under the sheets. She is holding Astrid as she feeds her, curled against her chest.

I try not to stare. It's the first time Astrid has been quiet, except when she's sleeping, which doesn't feel often. The girl has a set of lungs on her. She probably gets that from her mother.

There are boxers in the top drawer of my dresser. I stalk across the room, the towel snug around my waist. The bullet that grazed my leg was superficial. It doesn't hurt, but that could also be the narcotics prescribed, making me feel like I'm floating on air.

I drop my towel and dress.

Olivia glances at me. She opens her mouth but shuts it.

"What's that?" I ask. She doesn't say anything, but she was contemplating it, and I want to know what she's thinking.

"I didn't know about all the scars," she says as she glances over my back.

Quite a few injuries left a mark, from bullet wounds to literally being stabbed in the back.

"There's quite a lot we don't know about each other." I don't mean to come off sharp and abrasive, it just happens naturally.

I slide on my boxers and sweatpants, coming to sit at the edge of the bed. I skip the shirt.

"With Luka dead, you're safe. No one will harm you. I promise you're under my protection, whether you decide to stay with us or leave."

She's silent and glances from me down to Astrid as the little tiger falls asleep.

I shift closer, my arm nudging hers as I sit with her on the bed. "But if you leave, Astrid remains here, with me." I want to make it clear she can leave at any time, but not with my daughter.

"Do you want me here as Astrid's mother?" she asks. "Or are you looking for more with me?"

Her cheeks redden, and she smiles weakly, staring down at the bedsheets.

I brush a lock of hair from her eyes, pushing it behind her ear.

Timidly, she glances at me.

Is she embarrassed talking about what we shared?

It was sex. Hot and fun, but there wasn't anything more to it. She had a hormonal need, and I scratched that itch.

Right?

"What we shared, it was wonderful, but it was just to satisfy you while you were pregnant," I say, reminding her of the agreement.

Primal.

Scorching.

Amazing sex.

I'd never been jealous before Olivia. I also had never desired a long-term relationship or a commitment of any kind.

"Has that changed for you?" I ask, staring into her pale blue gaze. Sometime between being friends with benefits and having a kid, I crave more. Companionship. "Because I selfishly want you here with me. You know my darkest secrets, that I'm a mafia don. Do you still want to be with me?" I ask, leaving the choice up to her.

I'd never force myself on her. It's a choice that she must make, whether this life is what she wants to be a part of with Astrid and me.

It's dark.

Dangerous.

And can lead to loss and heartache, but it's worth it to me.

I wouldn't fault her for wanting a normal life, a quiet and fresh start with no reminder of her past and the damage I've caused along the way.

"I do, but I don't want to be locked in a bedroom forced to follow orders from your guards."

Does she not see that I kept her here to keep her safe?

"It was only for your protection while we attacked the Caruso family. You aren't a hostage. You can come and go as you please. However, I would like to keep a security detail on you. Mafia or not, I'm still a billionaire, and that comes with trouble following me around."

She presses a soft, chaste kiss to my cheek. "Are you sure you're not insisting on a guard to spy on me?"

I'm not sure whether she's joking or serious. "I wouldn't do that," I say.

"Good," she says, handing Astrid over to me. "You should burp her and change her diaper, Daddy."

I pin her with my stare. "Daddy?"

"What? Do you prefer she calls you papa or don?" Olivia smirks.

"Daddy is fine, but I'm not your Daddy."

Olivia snorts and rolls her eyes. "You'd better not be. I don't need you giving me timeouts or putting me in the corner for misbehaving." She sticks out her tongue at me playfully.

Is this what I have to look forward to, her teaching our daughter how to be a little brat around here?

I take Astrid from her embrace and grab the baby rag, putting it over my shoulder while I burp the little tyke. She's growing fast. Every day, I fall even more in love with her. How is that possible?

"Thank you," I say.

"You won't be thanking me for long." Olivia glances at me with a grin. "Don't forget to change her diaper," she says and wrinkles her nose. "That kid knows how to leave a stinky trail."

"Thank you for giving me Astrid," I clarify. I wasn't thanking her for handing over my kid with a poopy diaper.

She didn't have to agree to be a surrogate.

Sure, the payday is nice, but after all she'd been through, she could have walked away or fought for custody and destroyed my life and my reputation.

EPILOGUE

THREE YEARS LATER

OLIVIA

"Look, Daddy!" Astrid squeals as she runs to Jace, carrying the pregnancy stick that she stole from the bathroom.

The kid has impeccable timing.

I'd chase after her, but she's like a bolt of lightning, and she's already made her announcement. Not just in front of Jace, but a half dozen of his finest men.

"What do we have here?" Jace asks, a smile on his face as he holds out his hand for Astrid to hand him the stick.

I stand awkwardly at the door of his office.

Shit.

This is not how I intended to tell him.

I didn't even really consider how I would announce the news that we were pregnant with our second child.

"Gentlemen, can you give us a moment?" Jace asks.

They clear out of the room, one by one. A small part of me wants to dash with them, leave Jace and Astrid to figure out how to read the stick while I get some ice cream and then take a nap.

He pulls Astrid onto his lap.

Jace always looks like a businessman with his perfectly tailored suit. He doesn't seem to care that Astrid's dress has a dash of honey on the front. Keeping the kid clean has been one hell of a task.

"Did you tell Astrid before me?" Jace asks. He doesn't seem upset, just perplexed that his daughter came running into his office unannounced.

"No, and I certainly didn't want you to find out like this in front of all your men," I say, stepping farther into his office.

Jace laughs and leans back in his chair. "That's not all my men. But they are my finest and most dedicated employees. Present company excluded."

"I haven't worked for you for three years," I say, reminding him that I chose the family over the job.

Looking after Astrid is a full-time job, so is keeping her safe. I couldn't trust a nanny to do that with our daughter. Not when Jace is worth billions. There are too many people who would take advantage of him, or who could hurt our little girl.

Besides, in my free time, I get the opportunity to paint. I've been fortunate enough to sell a handful of canvases. Not that we need the money, but it feels good to accomplish one of my dreams.

"So, it's official?" he asks, gesturing toward the pregnancy stick. "How many did you take?"

Does he really think it's a false positive? It's not like we've been careful lately. Now that we're married, we haven't worried about protection. And he's made it known that he wants a son.

Like I have a choice in the matter of the sex of the baby.

"I took enough of them to know either their quality control is crap, or I'm having a baby."

"Yay!" Astrid's eyes widen, and she claps excitedly. "I get to be a big sister or a big brother!"

Jace chuckles and gives her several kisses on her cheek. "You will be a big sister," he says. "We won't know if the baby is a boy or a girl for several months."

"Oh." Astrid's brow furrows, confused. She hops down from Jace's lap and hurries to the door. "Can I have cookies?"

"One," I say.

The house is secure, safe for a little girl to run around without worrying about any danger. She slips out of the office and dashes down the hallway as her soft patter of footsteps hurry to the kitchen.

Jace holds out his arms, and I gracefully fall onto his lap, my arms around his neck. "Are you ready for a second kid?" I ask.

"Are you?" He leans closer, his breath teases my ear. "Remember all those dirty dreams you used to have of me while you were pregnant with Astrid?"

I rest my forehead against his. How could I forget? "Oh, I remember. I also recall the doctor giving us advice about positions."

"Yeah, we won't need her advice this time around," Jace says with a wide grin. "I know how to satisfy my wife."

———

Thank you for reading Unwilling Vow. I hope you enjoyed Olivia and Jace's story.

Want more from the Mafia Marriages series? One-click Ruthless Vow for a steamy, slow-burn romance that brings all your favorite mafia men from the series together!

Men say I'm bred with Russian, that I should be Bratva.

I have a reputation as being the most vicious and ruthless Italian in the world. They're not wrong.

I murdered my boss and stole his throne.

He made me the beast that I am, and I made him pay the price.

But there's a girl I want beside me while I rule the city.

The only problem, she's Russian and the little sister of my enemy. She's innocent, naive, and has no idea what I intend to do to her family.

We're at war with the Bratva...

They've threatened our women, children and attempted to burn our homes to the ground. They've come after our organization, stolen our shipments, and forced our hand.

The dons and our most trusted men must come together to Chicago to destroy the Bratva.

This secret baby, steamy, slow-burn romantic suspense is the fifth book in the Mafia Marriages series. While it is a standalone, it features the mafia men of the previous books and will be enjoyed even more if you've read the entire series.

One-click Ruthless Vow!

GIVEAWAYS, FREE BOOKS, AND MORE GOODIES

I hope you enjoyed Unwilling Vow and loved Olivia and Jace's story.

Sign up for my Willow Fox newsletter

If you enjoyed Unwilling Vow, please take a moment to leave a review. Reviews helps other readers discover my books.

Not sure what to write? That's okay. It doesn't have to be long. You can share how you discovered my book; was it a recommendation by a friend or a book club? Let readers know who your favorite character is or what you'd like to see happen next.

Thank you for reading! I hope you'll consider joining my mailing list for free books, promotions, giveaways, and new release news.

ABOUT THE AUTHOR

Willow Fox has loved writing since she was in high school (many ages ago). Her small town romances are reflective of living in a small town in rural America.

Whether she's writing romance or sitting outside by the bonfire reading a good book, Willow loves the magic of the written word.

She dreams of being swept off her feet and hopes to do that to her readers!

Visit her website at:

https://authorwillowfox.com

ALSO BY WILLOW FOX

Dangerous Boss

Bossy Single Dad Series

Billionaire Grump

Mountain Grump

Bachelor Grump

Faking it with the Billionaire

Looking for kinkier books? Try these spicy stories written under the name Allison West.

Boxsets

Academy of Littles

Western Daddies Collection

Obey Daddy Collection

The Alpha Collection

Western Daddies

Her Billionaire Daddy

Her Cowboy Daddy

Her Outlaw Daddy

Her Forbidden Daddy

Standalone Romances

The Victorian Shift

Jailed Little Jade

Prefer a sweeter romance with action and adventure?
Check out these titles under the name Ruth Silver.

Aberrant Series

Love Forbidden

Secrets Forbidden

Magic Forbidden

Escape Forbidden

Refuge Forbidden

Boxsets

Gem Apocalypse

Nightblood

Royal Reaper

Royal Deception

Standalones

Stolen Art